I0748382

NECROMANTIC

and other illustrated nightmares

Written by Katherine Kitchener
Illustrated by Carlos Sánchez (Dood)

NECROMANTIC

For information contact :
katherinekitchener55@gmail.com

Cover and interior art by Carlos Sánchez
Book and Cover design by Katherine Kitchener
ISBN: 978-0-6487454-0-2

First Edition: March 2020

10 9 8 7 6 5 4 3 2 1

For Evan and Leo

With special thanks to Anthony, Gretchen and Christian

CONTENTS

FOREWORD

IN AUSTRALIA IN ABOUT the mid-nineties there was a kids' TV show called 'The Book Place'. I was probably a little old for it, but I would still sometimes watch, particularly if I was home sick from school.

The show was presided over by a grotesque little puppet named 'Book Worm'. Book Worm was a fat, stubby little thing, his body pinkish-brown and segmented. His head was topped with fuzzy little protrusions that were presumably meant to be antennae, but that looked more like the ossicones on a giraffe. He wore nothing save a shirt-collar and a tie... or maybe it was a bow-tie.

I can't remember if the show's titular 'place' was supposed to be a library or a book store (I don't remember there being patrons, either way) but it was certainly a cosy place that, in addition to Book Worm, was peopled with a small cast of live-action humans, all with soft, rich voices, in contrast to Book Worm's quavering, child-like tones.

In each episode, different cast members would take turns reading aloud from the myriad picture books that the place was full of. There would be maybe three or so books read in an episode and, as I recall, the books read in each episode would all be centred around a common theme.

There is one story in particular that stuck with me, although I can't remember the title or the author. What I remember is Book Worm sitting on the arm of the reading chair, staring into the camera with his black, glassy eyes – his gaping, toothless mouth set in a permanent, gummy smile – as one of his friends (Co-workers? Handlers? Puppeteers?) held the book aloft. This human prop dutifully turned pages as Book Worm – in a breathy, tremulous voice – narrated a story about an unremarkable little boy who made a pact with some unseen sea monster who offered the boy the ability to paint as long as he promised to paint the sea. The boy, naturally, broke his promise and it seemed he would get away with it, until a hideous creature started to appear in all his paintings.

"That doesn't sound very much like a children's story," my mother responded when I recounted the tale. I frowned. She should know, having run 'storytime' at our local library for years. But still, "I remember it so clearly" I insisted.

"If you remember it so clearly, then why don't you have a title? Or an author?" she replied reasonably. "Maybe you just dreamt it? You always did have a vivid imagination."

My frown deepened. I had considered that possibility myself dozens of times, though I resisted the idea.

I had been trying to track the story down for years, on and off. Ever since my early teens. In the pre-Google days I would ask my classmates if they ever remembered such a story from their own childhoods, but no one did. Every time I visited a public library I would pick through the children's book collection, hoping for some serendipitous encounter. Later, I tried online message boards and chat-rooms.

I even found a few that were specifically aimed at helping people remember the titles of half-forgotten books.

My quest led me down the path of examining other incongruous childhood memories that I could find no logical place for in my own narrative, or in the shared history of family and friends. I started turning to my dreams, some of which I remembered with more clarity than the vaguely remembered childhood anecdotes that floated at the outskirts of my conscious mind.

I never did find the book, and instead felt compelled to write my own, so please join me in the following pages as I try to remember my nightmares and to construct bad dreams out of stray memories.

NECROMANTIC

YOU HAVE NO IDEA what you are doing, that much is obvious. You burst in, with your too-bright jewellery and your too-wide grin and stride up to the bar – loudly ordering a beer even though everyone else is drinking spiced rum.

Barely half a drink in and you begin boasting, to anyone who will listen, of how far you have travelled and how much danger you have faced to get here – how you proved to be too smart and too quick and too strong for those that tried to thwart you.

When she approaches you from the

other end of the bar in a cloud of fragrance we all avert our eyes, but you gaze at her steadily and flash a smile that is like a bolt of lightning in that dark room. You offer to buy her a drink and she accepts. You turn to the barkeep but he is already bringing the drink over – something dark and sanguine in a crystal glass. You arch an eyebrow. "Wine?" you ask. "Pomegranate juice." she corrects, then takes a sip of the tartly sweet fluid, her eyes not leaving yours.

You lower your voice, then, speaking to her in something more like a purr. You bat long eyelashes over eyes that gleam like two shards of obsidian. We all watch you and grind our teeth but you seem not to notice, or else you don't care. You are probably used to being looked at. You with your smooth, dark complexion, your long, elegant neck and your hair, a galaxy of glossy spirals.

In contrast, her skin is pale and slightly transparent, like the belly of a fish. Upon her breasts is a delicate tracery of little, blue veins. Like lace-work. Like rivulets. With a boldness that makes us shake our heads in disgust you trace one of those lines along her collarbone. She sighs and parts her juice-stained lips.

As she speaks to you, her voice a soft, funereal whisper, her hands flutter about like a pair of tiny doves. On closer inspection you see that her nails, though neatly trimmed and freshly painted, are lined with dirt. The scent you had first taken to be perfume is actually embalming fluid and it doesn't quite cover that other, darker scent that clings to her – the sickly mixture of dried blood and wet clay.

Why did you come? Was it the promise of riches that drew you here? It's true that she has wealth beyond imagining – a miser's hoard. Perhaps you dreamt of making use of her power to hurt your enemies, or of obtaining that power for yourself. Or maybe you just wanted to be able to say that you had been here, that you had touched the hem of her skirt, that she had spoken your name.

Little does it matter, in the end, whether you came for money, for revenge, for fame. It always ends the same way. Perhaps you think it will be different for you – because you are brave and pure-hearted or because you are a woman – but to her you are no different to the rest of us. In the end you're only meat and bone.

*

We do not have to be there to know what happens next.

She leads you through the silver night to the nearby cemetery. It, and the bar you left us in, are all that remains of the town that once stood here. Perhaps some of us lived here back then - had families, worked the land - but, if so, we do not remember. It is as though we never existed before we loved her.

The grounds of the cemetery are remarkably, almost obsessively, well-kept, but perhaps you do not notice this. She laughs girlishly as she picks her way spryly through a labyrinth of tombstones and statuary – a whole host of marble angels, their cold and perfect features a faint echo of hers.

This journey is familiar to all of us. We have each played it over in our heads every night since – the cool air, the bright, full moon, her figure ahead flitting between the graves towards the white mausoleum that dominates those grounds. She was like some exquisite moth. A pale and delicate nocturnal creature. If only we had known, as we followed her through the night, that it was we who were the moths and she, the flame.

The door to the crypt is open and she waits for you there in a sliver of moonlight. About the entrance is a cluster of pomegranate trees. Those fruits, plump and bursting with bright red seeds, form the beating heart of the cemetery. You finally catch up and she leads you down a narrow set of stairs into her sanctum.

The main chamber is lit by a mass of candles. You are naïve enough to think them beeswax, but we know with what grim precision she crafted them from rarer tallow. Adipocere drips off them to form greasy pools on the cold, marble floor. Cut flowers are displayed in urns – gardenia, camellia and lilies, of course. You wonder, only fleetingly, how she keeps them so fresh. All of them are plump and radiant with life in a way that is almost obscene in those sepulchral surrounds.

She moves to the far end of the chamber where, behind a low, flat table, a large open fire does little to dispel the subterranean damp. She beckons for you to join her.

Run. That's what you should do; what we all silently urge you to do. While the table lies between the two of you, you should turn your back and bolt for the stairs and the crisp, fresh air of the outside world. You could still say you had been here. You could even snatch a flower on the way out as a memento. You don't run, though. Of course you don't.

You approach the stone table, your step perhaps a little less confident than before. She offers to read your fortune and you agree, expecting cards, but instead she brings forth a sack of old sheep bones and, laughing, tosses them one after another into the fire. The bones snap and fracture in the heat, revealing your life's journey in a series of cracks and fissures.

Leaning in close to the fire your hand brushes against hers. Perhaps it is an accident. Perhaps not. Either way, you are taken aback by how warm it is. "I had expected you to be cold," you confess. She turns to you then and peers at you almost shyly from behind the curtain of her fringe, "I can't be, with you here to keep me warm."

When you kiss her, her breath has the too-sweet taste of over-ripe fruit. But her lips, like her hands, are soft and warm and so you kiss her deeper still, gathering up her delicate frame in your arms and pulling her towards yourself. Her moans echo in the large chamber so that it sounds like she is all around you. Above you. Within you.
Eventually she pulls away and, reluctantly, you let her. She looks you in the eye and her pupils are like black holes, so wide they threaten to swallow her up. To swallow you both up. Taking your hands in hers she guides you down onto the stone table and

lays you out. You are reminded, irresistibly, of a sacrifice on an altar and for the first time you begin to feel something like fear. You watch, warily, as she steps back and slowly peels away her dusky robes. The flesh beneath is pale and smooth and glows like starlight.

You sit up and quickly remove your own clothes, tossing them onto the floor beside the fire. She kicks them aside.

"We won't be needing those," she says as she climbs upon the table to join you.

You have heard the phrase, 'the sweet embrace of death' but never before had you really thought about it. We know too well the similarities between a lover's embrace and the end of life – the shallow breath, the quickening pulse, the loss of self in one final, aching gasp. There, upon that stone table, you die a little.

Afterwards, as she lies curled like a fern beside you, you run your fingers through her fine, fair hair, lifting a strand up to your face and inhaling its perfume. It is the same bitter-sweet scent you noticed on her earlier – the same scent that pervades the whole chamber, but in a more concentrated form. You wonder if you will ever get the smell out of your own clothes and hair. You won't.

She sits up and slips her robes back

on then, picking up a nearby candelabra, beckons to you. "I have something to show you." She turns and walks away. You dress yourself, clumsy in your haste, and stumble after her.

She leads you to a narrow passage. Beyond the passage is another set of stairs leading further downwards. You follow her deeper underground into a crypt below the crypt. A charnel house where the cloying sweetness of the chamber above – the smell of incense and embalming fluid – gives was to a putrescence that stings you eyes and forces you to cover your nose and mouth with your arm. "What is this?" you ask, your voice muffled.

She says nothing, instead simply standing aside and motioning for you to pass her. For all your earlier bravado you step forward only reluctantly, and not without casting a wistful glance back behind you to the candlelit chamber above.

The charnel house is unlit, the only illumination coming from the flickering light she bears. You inch forwards, peering into the darkness to try and make out your surroundings. There is a tapping on your shoulder and you whirl around, but it is just her, of course, offering you the candelabra. You take it gratefully and return to your inspection.

As you turn back, now with the aid of the candlelight, you find yourself faced with a huge pile of corpses in various stages of decomposition. The corpses closest to the damp, stone walls are deliquescent – what remains of their bodies oozing onto the floor. At the bottom of the pile, and jutting out at various points throughout it, are a jumble of bones – some so old and dry they are turning to powder. The bodies that cap off that dreadful mound are so fresh and unmarred they may just have been sleeping, although the stench suggests otherwise.

Your heart pounds heavily and you desperately try to assess your situation. She is standing between you and the only exit, but she is not a large woman. You take a deep breath, trying to steady your nerves, then turn back to face her. You force a smile, "Who are they? Your old lovers?"

"Some of them." she replies coolly, without a trace of irony. You reach then for your weapon, only to realise you have left it on the floor in the chamber above.

"Oh no, my love," she coos like a dove and takes one graceful step towards you, "Don't fear." she leans forward and blows out the candles, "I could never part from you."

*

The next evening you return to us but – ah! How changed! Silently you take your place beside us (we have already made room). The barkeeper, without looking up, pours another glass of rum.

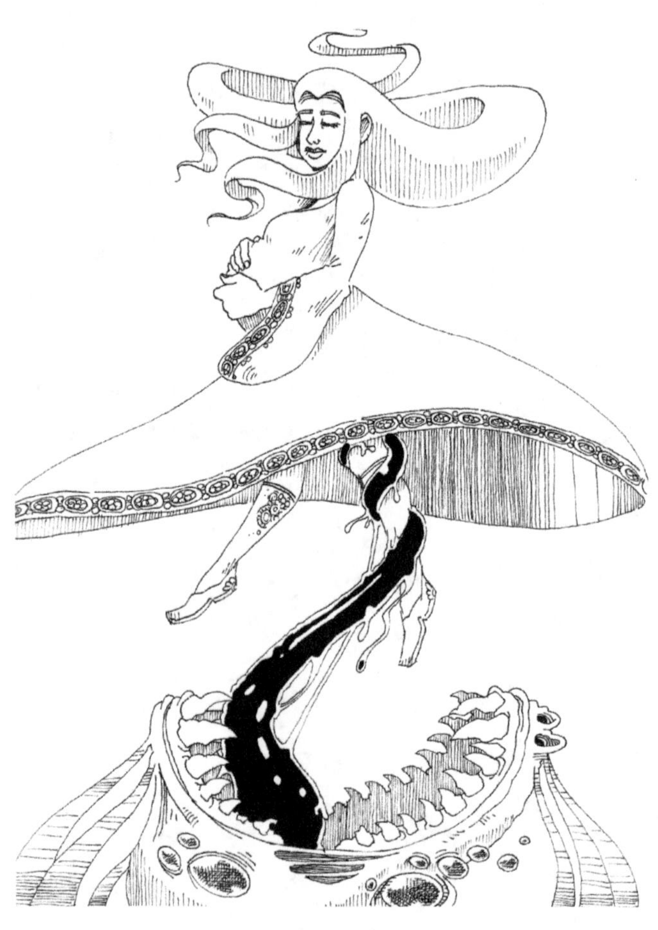

ANOTHER HUNGRY MOUTH

CONSTANCE WOULD NOT tell anyone who the father was. Not when her mother cried nor when her father yelled. Not even when her older sister, Emily, sat on her bed and held her in her arms – rocking her gently.

Constance was four-months pregnant when she told her family, and already beginning to show. Emily was furious at herself for not picking up on the signs earlier – the baggy clothes Constance had taken to wearing in lieu of her usual tailored look, her out-of-control appetite, her strange secretiveness. It all seemed so obvious, now.

Still, how could anyone have been expected to guess this? This was Constance, after all. Constance the meekly obedient, Constance the prim and proper, Constance the chronically shy. She was supposed to be the good daughter!

And then, of course, there was that other thing.

"But I thought you didn't even like boys." Emily pressed. Constance wrinkled her nose in distaste, "I don't," she replied emphatically. "...But I wouldn't exactly call them a 'boy'," she added with a sly smile.

Emily jerked away in shock, "What!?"

Constance lifted a hand up to her mouth to stifle a giggle.

"How old is this guy?" Emily asked, unable to keep the stern edge out of her voice.

"I — I don't know." Constance confessed and, her smile suddenly fading, began to wring her hands. "Pretty old, I think."

"You 'think'?"

Constance shrugged.

"Connie...who—?"

"No!" Constance suddenly yelled, startling Emily. Constance reached out and clasped Emily's hands tightly in her own,

"Emily," she pleaded, "Don't ask me that. Please. I swore I'd never tell."

Emily snatched her hands away. She could feel anger rising in her throat like bile. "Connie, if you're protecting some creep—"

Constance laughed. Emily didn't see what was so funny.

"It's not like that," she insisted when her fit of giggles subsided, "It's more like..." she paused and stared off somewhere into the middle-distance over Emily's shoulders, "It's like... have you ever had a secret that you didn't want to tell anyone because it would make it less... special? Less 'yours'?"

Emily nodded slowly, although she wasn't at all sure that she had. Wasn't part of the fun of having a secret in telling it to somebody?

"It's like that," Constance continued. "This belongs to me, and I don't want to share it with anybody."

"Not even me?" Emily wheedled, but Constance just continued to stare at nothing, a soft smile playing at the corners of her mouth.

*

The last few months leading up to

Constance's confinement were tense, to say the least. Constance's condition could not be kept a secret for long and, in the way of small towns, once one person found out, the news spread like a virus – persistent and insidious. Rumours abounded about the identity of the father. Her schoolmates, her teachers, and her doctor all had gleefully accusatory fingers pointed in their direction. No male with any link to Constance was exempt.

One particularly malicious gossip suggested that Constance would not talk about the father because it was her own father. When Emily heard this rumour she tracked it back to its source – a pimply little boy in year 8 – and delivered one devastating punch to his blemished features, earning herself a week's suspension and the boy a bloodied nose and split lip.

Things were even more strained at home. Dinners had become a silent affair with neither of their parents so much as glancing up from their plates to look at Constance. Emily had to grit her teeth in rage that the familial bond that linked parents and daughters could have proven to be so weak.

What surprised Emily more than anything, though, was how unfazed Constance seemed to be by all of this.

Where every whispered slur or raised eyebrow caused Emily to bristle, Constance breezed through her days with head held high as though completely oblivious to the shame that her family felt. Shame that people expected her to feel as well. Amidst all the murk and mire and casual cruelty, Constance positively glowed. Emily had never loved her sister more.

*

When the child arrived and Emily was finally allowed in to visit she was dumbstruck. There was Constance – sweaty and tired-eyed but beaming – and in her arms a tiny, wrinkled form: "James." Constance informed her without looking up.

The fact that her little sister, her own Connie, had created this tiny person as though from nothing filled Emily with a quiet awe.

When Constance finally tore her love-struck gaze from her new baby and looked up, Emily saw that her sister's eyes were filmed with tears and she felt a lump rise in her own throat. The sisters' eyes locked and they were both overcome with a joy so bright and intense that it seemed like it would last forever.

It did not.

'Failure to thrive' was the term the paediatrician used, and what it amounted to was that, despite apparently feeding normally, James was not putting on any weight. In fact, over the next twelve weeks James continued to drop weight until he was well below his birth weight.

They ran all kinds of tests. Emily accompanied her sister and nephew to what seemed like an endless cycle of doctor's offices and waiting rooms and consulting suites, where sympathetic people with stethoscopes about their necks spoke in hushed tones of things like 'caloric retention' and 'metabolic demand'. All Constance ever seemed able to say in response was, "Oh."

As days passed all Emily could do was watch as her sister grew paler and more anxious. As James lost weight Constance, too, seemed to diminish. She became absent-minded and vague – forgetting tasks part way through and often trailing off mid-sentence. She withdrew into herself until she had little more substance than her own shadow. Emily wanted to help Constance, but it was like she could no longer reach her. With every day Constance sank deeper and deeper into some dark pit and, however hard she tried, Emily just couldn't follow her.

All the tests came back negative, and with every result Emily saw relief fighting with anxiety in her sister's drawn face. So James didn't have cystic fibrosis or diabetes or hyperthyroidism... but was what was wrong with him?

*

Emily was not sure what had woken her up. She lay there for some time in the early morning chill, staring blankly at the ceiling while a sense of dread slowly crept up on her. What started as a feeling of discomfort in her belly slowly turned into a dull thudding in her breast.

It was then that she noticed the sickly yellow light seeping in under her bedroom door. She rolled over to face the glow and noticed, as she did, that her alarm clock displayed 2.15am. Too late for her parents, and too early for Constance, surely.

Reluctantly, Emily dragged her sleep-heavy body out of bed and shuffled toward her bedroom door. When she opened it she saw that the source of the light was not one of the other bedrooms but, rather, the kitchen across the hallway. Grumbling to herself, Emily made her shambling progress towards the kitchen where she found the fridge door wide open and humming slightly. Still groggy, she noticed that the fridge's contents were in a state of disarray. The leftovers were uncovered, crumbs littered the bottom shelf and someone had spilled the milk. Closing the door she made her way back to her bedroom.

Halfway down the hallway, Emily halted as she heard a noise coming from Constance's room – a soft susurration. She recognised her sister's voice, but the pitch was too low for her to make out the words. Something in the tone of the voice emanating from the darkness of Constance's room—a wheedling note edged with a quiet urgency—stayed Emily and brought back the creeping dreaded that had first dragged her from her slumber.

"Connie?" Emily asked anxiously as she opened the door. When she heard no response, just a continuation of Constance's hushed whispers, Emily flicked on the light.

Constance was bent over James' crib. It was several minutes before she straightened up and, blinking at the light, turned to face her sister.

Emily stifled her own cry of surprise when she saw Constance's face. The young girl's eyes were bloodshot from lack of sleep and dark rings hang below them. It was not this that took Emily aback, however, but the expression in those strained eyes. A startled, trapped look almost feral in its intensity flickered across Constance's eyes, rendering the familiar features alien to Emily.

It was Constance who broke the silence. "He won't eat." she said to Emily, her tone desperate. "I don't know what he eats!"

Emily's eyes darted down, then, and she saw that her sister was clutching something tightly in her right hand – a lumpy mass that dripped on the rug. So incongruous was the sight that Emily did not immediately register what it was... a raw steak. Emily stared in mute shock while her mind reeled. What was Constance doing with that meat? What was she thinking?

Emily swallowed a lump in her throat and then began, slowly and with soothing noises, to advance on Constance. "Shh, Connie," she crooned gently. "Shh..."

When Emily reached her younger sister she took Connie's trembling hands into her own, surreptitiously removing the slab of meat and placing it on the changing table. She glanced down into the crib and noted that James was sleeping soundly.

Gently she guided Constance back to her

bed and persuaded her to lie down. Once she was beneath the covers, Constance began to weep softly. "I don't know what he eats," she choked out between sobs.

Emily stayed seated on the edge of her sister's bed and stroked her long, dark hair until she fell asleep.

*

That feeling of uneasiness stayed with Emily all through the next day. It was Saturday and her friends wanted to go to the movies, but she blew them off. Her parents were both away for the weekend and the idea of sitting there in the dark while Constance stayed home alone with James was intolerable to Emily.

Instead she spent the entire day just hanging around the house, unable to commit herself to any activity for more than a few minutes. She found herself hovering around Constance and watching her critically. She could not seem to get out of her head that image of Constance standing over James' crib with the lights out clutching a chunk of meat.

For her part, Constance behaved as if the previous night had not happened at all. She changed James and bathed him. She gave him his formula and even played with him on the lounge room floor – tickling his feet and blowing raspberries on his too-flat tummy. She would lift him up in the air and kiss his middle almost as if, for a moment, at least, she did not notice the worrying concave of her son's belly.

As Emily watched Constance, however, she could not keep herself from thinking that her sister's smile looked strangely painted on and that there was something more than just fatigue behind her red-rimmed eyes.

Emily slept fitfully that night. Her sleep was disturbed by strange nightmares that, although she forgot their content almost immediately after she awoke, left her feeling shaky and disoriented.

When a sudden wail from James pierced the night Emily immediately sat bolt upright, then propelled herself out of bed before she had even registered what the sound was. She had heard James cries often enough to be familiar with them, could even tune them out most nights, but they were different this time. These cries were much, much louder than normal, but also strangely... wet.

Emily threw the door to Constance's room open. "Connie, what's wrong?" she gasped, feeling like she may choke on her own heart. She was in such a rush she forgot to switch on the light as she charged through the door and towards her sister "I heard—"

"Oh!" came Constance's startled cry as she dropped something.

"What... what have you done?" Emily whispered when she saw the bloody kitchen knife on the floor. She took a step toward Constance, then turned and ran up to the crib, where James had suddenly stopped his piercing wails. Emily, shaking now, stared down at her nephew.

There was a red jagged line that ran along the child's belly – starting at the base of his throat and running all the way down to below his navel. To Emily's horror the gash began to gape, exposing a bloody, red interior out of which protruded the shattered remnants of James' rib cage – now just jagged fragments of bone.

"Oh my god, Connie. What have you done?"

Emily braced herself against the side of the crib as she fought off waves of nausea and disbelief.

She felt her head spin and her vision begin to blur as her breath caught in her throat, but still she could not tear her eyes away from her nephew's twisted form.

After what seemed an interminable time Emily's breath returned to her, though it was shallow and ragged. As her vision cleared and adjusted to the faint light that filtered in from the open curtain she realised that she had made a mistake. In her initial shock Emily had thought the white shards in James' split torso to be ribs, but now she saw that this was not the case at all. They were teeth.

Great, jagged teeth set in a crooked, sideways mouth than ran most of the length of James' tiny body. As Emily watched, that terrible nether-mouth began to gape again, wider this time, and from out of its impossible depths snaked a black, slimy tendril that could only be a tongue.

Letting out a strangled cry, Emily stumbled backward then watched as the tongue rose up and out of the crib, flailing back and forth as though tasting the air. The tongue reached all the way to the changing table and began to tap on its surface.

It was only then that Emily saw a fuzzy mound lying on the changing table, it's head crudely cut off.

As Emily watched, the tongue slowly slid towards the inert rodent and then, with horrible deftness, wrapped around it and lifted it off the table, pulling it back towards the crib and the terrible, waiting maw. The tongue made a wet, slurping noise as it retreated back behind the crooked fangs.

From somewhere behind Emily came a weak cry of “Oh!” Emily had forgotten Constance was even there.

Emily turned and saw Constance standing there, her hands clasped so tightly together that the knuckles were white. Her moist, febrile eyes glittered in the dim light. Emily saw that there was no fear in those eyes. Only wonder.

“Oh, Emily!” Constance sighed rapturously, “He looks *just* like his father!”

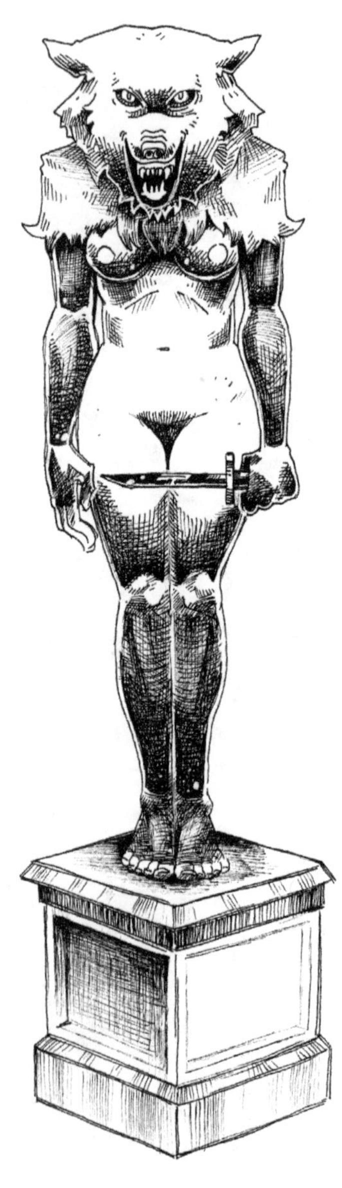

STATUESQUE

"YOU MISSED THE turn-off." Stephanie announced in her usual, strident tone. "Mm-hmm," Cara responded as she clenched her hands tighter still around the steering wheel and stared fixedly at what little of the road ahead was illuminated by the car's headlights.

"No fucking shit," is what she really wanted to say, but there was no way she would do that, and risk another lecture from Stephanie about the 'gradual degradation of the English language' with a side helping of 'youth today' and some poorly concealed barbs about Cara's own level of maturity.

Cara clenched her teeth, silently wondering where things had gone wrong.

When she and Stephanie had first started dating, Cara's friends and relatives alike had objected. She had just got out of a bad relationship and everyone seemed to think she was rushing into things too soon. The age difference, too, at over twenty years, raised more than a few eyebrows. It did not help that Cara's sexuality, something she had only become open about in recent years, still didn't sit well with her parents. Her father hid behind awkward jokes, whereas her mother would go all stiff and 'uncomfortable' whenever the topic of girlfriends came up.

But Cara ignored these criticisms, and, some may say, her own better-judgement. Stephanie was exciting – mature and elegant. Cara found the older woman's intelligence and assertiveness challenging. She was flattered, too, that someone with as much experience and beauty as Stephanie could show any interest in her – a mousy woman in her late twenties who had only just moved out of her parents' home.

The holiday had been Cara's own idea. A road trip up to the Border Ranges to explore the rainforest then a jaunt to Byron Bay to soak up the summer sun – just the two of them. She had been a little shy when first suggesting the idea to Stephanie, but was gratified by how readily her girlfriend accepted. Stephanie didn't drive, herself. It was bad for the environment, she said, and unessential for someone living right in the Melbourne CBD. Still, she had no qualms about the idea of being chauffeured about by Cara. Cara didn't mind either. In fact, she was secretly pleased that she had found a way to make herself useful to Stephanie.

Her parents had tried to forbid the trip once they found out about it but Cara, for once, stood her ground. She was an adult now and what she did with her life and who she spent her time with was her own business.

“We just want what's best for you!” insisted her mother, anxiously wringing her hands as Cara loaded up the boot of her car with the camping supplies she had stored in her parents' garage.

“You barely know her!” chastised her best friend, Jo, as they shared a farewell drink at their favourite bar.

Cara ignored them all. She wasn't going to be pressured or bullied into doing what everyone expected of her. She had found the woman she loved and she wasn't going to let anything deter her from the adventure she and Stephanie had planned together.

Once they began their journey it did not take long for things to deteriorate. The long hours spent driving were more tiring than Cara had anticipated, particularly with Stephanie in the passenger seat beside her complaining about everything from the temperature to the scenery to Cara's driving, in her loud, clipped tones. Stephanie's posh accent, which made her sound almost British, was starting to grate on Cara's nerves after a couple of days on the road. What had seemed, at first, so sophisticated and refined now struck Cara as pretentious and annoying.

The truth was, the two women really had little in common apart from the few passionate nights they had spent together in Stephanie's inner-city apartment, and the more time they spent together the more obvious grew the gulf between them. Cara was not sure what stung more – the extinguishing of the fire that had burnt so brightly or the knowledge that her family and friends had been right all along.

Worst of all they were stuck together. Stuck in this car. Stuck on this interminable road trip. Stuck and hopelessly lost somewhere in the rainforests of northern New South Wales...or had they crossed over into Queensland? Where had she gone wrong?

"You're going around in circles," observed Stephanie and it was a moment before Cara realised she was referring to the road and not her own brooding thoughts. "I'm not!" Cara replied defensively, although in all honesty she could not be completely sure. The truth was the roads through that hilly region were so serpentine Cara had long since lost her sense of direction.

Up ahead, just to the side of the road, a large structure was gradually coming in to view. Cara cried out triumphantly, "Ah-ha! We can't be going around in circles. We haven't passed that statue before!"

The statue was gigantic, at least twenty feet tall. It showed a nude woman standing perfectly erect. Cara guessed by the fullness and pertness of the statue's bust that it was supposed to depict a relatively young woman, perhaps, like herself, somewhere in her twenties. It was impossible to say this with any accuracy, though. The face certainly gave no clue, for the woman's head was that of a giant she-wolf, it's fearsome muzzle frozen in a permanent snarl. The fur of the wolf-head ran down the shoulders of the woman and partially covered her breasts – an elegant, if vaguely unsettling, merging of woman and beast.

"What do you suppose it's made

of?" Stephanie pondered aloud. Without thinking, Cara responded, "Bronze," then immediately regretted it.

Stephanie let out her dry, bark of a laugh. "Bronze?" she scoffed, "Are you being serious? Out here in the middle of nowhere? Look how big that thing is! Do you know how much it would cost?"

"Oh, a million-billion dollars!" Cara snapped back facetiously.

Stephanie responded with another derisive snort, then crossed her arms and turned back to stare out of her own window again.

As the car pulled up close beside the statue, Cara noticed a small detail that had escaped her earlier. Although the woman was, indeed, completely nude, her right hand was clasped tightly around some small object. Cara slowed the car and peered into the darkness, trying to make out the shape of the object. Then, the headlights glinted off the long, narrow shape and she saw it for what it was – a knife. There was something about that sliver of a blade and the hand that gripped it so tenaciously that fascinated Cara. She glanced up again at the wolf-woman's vicious, enraged countenance. "Same," she muttered under her breath.

"Pardon?" Stephanie responded, turning away from her window to throw an icy look in Cara's direction. “Nothing.” Cara mumbled sullenly, then tightened her grip on the steering wheel as she accelerated away from the statue.

For another half hour or so the pair continued their drive in silence. Eventually, Stephanie yawned conspicuously. “At this rate it will be daylight before we find somewhere to sleep.” She was right, of course. It was well past midnight now and it seemed they were still no closer to finding a camp-site or caravan park or anywhere they could reasonably pull the car aside, even. With another yawn, one Cara felt sure was faked, Stephanie shuffled in her seat before resting her head against the window and closing her eyes.

Cara leaned in close to the steering wheel and squinted her eyes, desperately scanning the roadside for any indication of where they were or what direction they should head in. Where were all the road-signs? Surely there should be something to guide tourists like themselves, but there was nothing. Nothing at all Cara realised with a flood of panic—no indication of speed-limits, no hazard signs warning of the winding roads ahead—nothing. They hadn't encountered any wildlife, either, for at least the last couple of hours. What was going on?

Cara was just about to voice her concerns when something up ahead caught her attention. “Is that...the same statue?” she asked.

“I told you you were going around in circles,” remarked Stephanie without opening her eyes.

“No, Steph, look!” urged Cara, slowing the car right down. “It's fallen over.” Stephanie sat up in her seat. Sure enough at the roadside ahead of them a large statue lay on the ground – it's square base pointed to the road; a prominent, lupine snout pointing skywards. “Shouldn't we have heard it fall?”

“That *is* strange.” allowed Stephanie before pausing and then laughing. The harsh, dry sound set Cara's teeth on edge, “And you actually thought it was bronze!”

Cara, her brow furrowed, pulled the car up at the side of the road and turned off the engine. “What are you doing now?” Stephanie groaned in exasperation.

“Something's not right,” Cara insisted, her eyes glued to the fallen statue. Something about it stirred up strange and ambivalent feelings in her breast. She felt the cold grasp of dread tightening around her heart, but something else, too. Something almost like anticipation.

“We don't need any more delays!”

Stephanie scolded but Cara ignored her girlfriend's snarky tone. Unbuckling her seatbelt, she finally responded, "I just want a closer look."

Despite the lateness of the hour, Cara found the air outside to be hot and oppressively muggy. "I feel like I'm going to drown!" she thought, then tittered to herself – the noise sounding thin in the darkness.

Cara approached the statue and walked around it to observe it from all angles. It certainly looked like the statue they had seen earlier. The wolf-woman had the same build and the same fearsome countenance. It did look like bronze, too, or some kind of metal, at least. Cara reached out a hand and was surprised to find the statue cool to the touch. She rested a flushed cheek against the wolf-woman's flank and sighed appreciatively.

Somewhere behind her came a loud honk as Stephanie impatiently beeped the car horn. At the sound Cara ground her teeth together and clenched her fists tight. As she made this gesture she was suddenly reminded of the statue's own hands. Hadn't they been clasped around a knife?

Cara looked at the statue's bare fist. She could have sworn the statue she'd passed earlier had been holding a knife in it's right hand. She circled back to the left-hand side of the statue and found that it too, though tightly clenched, was not holding anything.

So it wasn't the same statue, after all. Curious, Cara reached out a hand to stroke the statue's fist. She pulled back sharply when she encountered something wet and sticky. Cara looked with disgust at the dark streak on her hand. Tentatively she raised the hand to her nose to sniff at the substance, but all she could detect was a faint metallic tang.

At that moment a streak of moonlight pierced through the clouds and glinted off something small just beside the statue's empty hand. Cara crouched down to get a better look and found, barely visible in the dark night, an ordinary knife laying among the tall grass. Cara stared at the blade for a few bewildered moments before picking it up. It was, she realised, a perfect replica of the knife she had seen in the statue's grasp, though much smaller, of course. It was long and narrow, rather like a scalpel, and the thin handle fit comfortably in her hand. She held it aloft and turned it back and forth, admiring the way the moonlight glinted off the sharp edge. This was no kitchen knife or butcher's cleaver. This elegant blade was an instrument of precision.

An instrument of grace.

Another honk from the car broke Cara's reverie. She stood up and cast one final, longing look at the head of the statue. Without thinking about what she was doing, her eyes locked on to the wolf-woman's toothy maw, Cara tucked the handle of the knife into the waistband of her jeans and pulled her t-shirt down to cover the blade. When Cara got back to the car she found Stephanie sitting with arms crossed in front of her chest, one perfectly-manicured finger tapping out an impatient rhythm. "Well I hope that was enlightening," sniffed Stephanie.

Cara gave no response as she slid into her seat and buckled her seatbelt.

"Well," Stephanie pressed. "Did you find anything interesting?"

As she turned on the ignition Cara's typically mild features twisted into an uncharacteristic grin. In the pallid moonlight that slipped through the rainforest canopy the grin looked almost like a snarl.

HER MINIATURE HORSES

"DO THEY smell?" Michael asked and, before Mary had a chance to respond, he leant in close to her desk and sniffed audibly.

Mary flinched, then, trying to regain her composure, stammered "W-well... Not these... particular ones. B-but—"

"Strawberry Shortcake!" Michael barked, causing Mary to flinch again.

"S-sorry?"

"My sister had those toys when we were kids. *They* smelled."

"Y-yes." Mary affirmed, "Yes they did".

Mary tried to think of something more to say, but before she could gather her thoughts Michael flashed his trademark sneer and wandered back to his desk. Mary settled back into her chair. She couldn't help but feel vaguely affronted by the encounter. True, Michael had not actually touched her possessions, but surely there was such a thing an olfactory personal space and, if so, he had certainly invaded hers.

Besides, he had made her speak an untruth. The vintage My Little Pony toys Mary kept on her desk were not from any of the scented lines—the Perfume Puff ponies or the Candy-Cane ponies, for instance—but of course they smelled. Mary darted her eyes over to Michael's desk and, seeing him absorbed in some spreadsheets, quickly snatched up one of the ponies and brought it close to her face, inhaling deeply.

There it was! The familiarly sharp and vaguely sweet scent of soft, moulded plastic that never failed to have a calming influence on her. Mary resisted the hypothesis that this smell somehow 'transported her back to her childhood'. That was then and this was now, and the smell made her feel good about now. It was a clean smell. A pure smell. A smell that made her think, with pride, of the perfectly ordered and rather substantial collection of G1 ponies she kept at home in her apartment.

Whenever Mary felt low, thinking of her collection was always a comfort. Some collectors liked to display their ponies according to the specific line of which they were a part, some displayed theirs according to release date, or theme. Mary, however, liked to display her collection according to colour. Entering her pony room was like walking into the middle of a rainbow. That's how Mary liked to see it, at least. That room was her sanctuary, her temple, the one irrevocably good part of her whole world.

*

Mary scrolled through the latest sales listings on, 'My Little Pony Trading Post' and 'My Little Pony Arena', flicking expertly between multiple tabs. She wasn't looking for anything in particular. She had most of the rarer ponies already, including several 'Nirvana' ponies exclusive to international markets. But this weekly review of the sales threads had become something of a habit for her, as routine as doing the laundry or taking out the rubbish. She bookmarked a few listings—ponies she already had but that were in slightly better condition–and was about to call it quits for the night when a little flag popped up on one of the tabs she had open.

Mary seldom got direct messages on any of the sites she frequented. Although she was something of a fixture on them, she was never a social person and didn't take part in the swaps or attend any of the conventions. She was also vaguely cagey about her collection, not liking to advertise too widely the rarities she had amassed. Really, unless it was a response to a message she had sent someone about a pony they had for sale, Mary never got any direct messages at all. Which is why Mary was surprised to find the message alert pop up in her tab and, having clicked it, to see the subject line, "For the consummate collector only." Mary read on:

Pale_Rider:

Hi FeatheredFetlocks! I have come across a very rare item that I think will be of interest to you and will make a unique addition to your estimable collection. I have a cousin who owns several warehouses (I'm not at liberty to say where), and while they were disposing of some long abandoned stock he came upon something extremely special and, knowing my proclivities, sent it to me immediately. Now, I can't be certain as I've found no official record of this, but the item appears to be a prototype of the Fancy Swirl range of My Little Ponies

Mary gasped. Could it really be? The Fancy Swirl ponies, sometimes referred to by collectors as 'Celestial ponies' or 'Fairy Brights' were a space-themed line of four ponies for which promotional box art had been created (and was widely circulated online) but, as far as Mary knew, the toys themselves had never actually gone into production. For decades collectors had drooled over that one illustration of the proposed line, and many people had turned their hands to making customs of the set, but never had there been even the hint of a rumour that prototypes might exist. If this was genuine (and Mary realised that was a big 'if') she had to have it.

I know it sounds unbelievable, but it's true! The particular Fancy Swirl I have is Starswirl (the pink one). I'd love to keep her for myself, but I'm downsizing my collection and really need the extra cash (I'm expecting, and the due date is this September!). If you think you might be interested, please get in contact with me. Don't delay. If I don't hear from you in 24 hours, I'll go to the next name on my list.

The rest of the message consisted of various assurances as to the quality and provenance of the toy, followed by details such as shipping rates and the seller's preferred payment methods. At the very bottom of the message was a link to an image. Mary clicked it.

What she saw did not fill her with confidence. The photo was blurry, to say the least. All she could really make out was a pinkish, roughly pony-shaped blob with several protrusions sprouting from its head. It might have been a Fancy Swirl prototype. It might have been anything.

It was probably a scam. The seller hadn't even named a price. Curious about who she was dealing with, Mary clicked on the username, "Pale_Rider" but found they had made no previous posts in the forums. Another red flag, surely.

But, still... what if it was genuine? Mary chewed at her bottom lip as she gazed again at the grainy photo. If this was for real, it was perhaps her one chance to own a truly unique piece of My Little Pony history—virtually a museum-piece—the world's only known Fancy Swirl pony.

All at once Mary leaned forward in her seat and started punching deliberately at the keyboard:

> *FeatherdFetlocks:*
>
> *Hello Pale_Rider, Thank you very much for your message. You certainly have me intrigued! I was just wondering if you had any more photos as the one you linked to is a teeny bit difficult to make out? Also, what is your asking price? Congratulations on the baby, by the way.*

On reflection, Mary deleted this last sentence. She didn't want to invite any friendly overtures from this person. She thought it was best just to stick to business.

Mary sent her response then settled back in her chair. She wasn't sure if or when she would hear back from her mysterious seller. She didn't have to wonder for long though as within minutes she received another message alert:

Pale_Rider:

Hi FeatheredFetlocks. I knew you'd be the one! Unfortunately my camera is broken so I can't send you any more photos, but I promise she's much less blurry in real life. She's perfect, in fact. I accept payment via PayPal and, for you, I'm asking $500.

Mary sucked in her breath sharply. Five-hundred dollars was not a small amount of money, by any means, but she had spent more on ponies before. She was still concerned about the photo and the suspiciously convenient excuse of the broken camera but then, if she was paying via PayPal, what was the harm? If the pony never arrived, or if it arrived and was an obvious fake, she could always get the money back. With only a few more moments deliberation, Mary made her decision.

*

Slowly, reverently, she lifted the tiny pony out of its nest of packing foam. The plastic was firm in her grasp but velvety soft to the touch. Mary examined her latest acquisition with an expert eye, running her hands over its surface to check for imperfections and peering closely to check for the tiny flecks of black age spots that collectors sometimes called 'pony cancer'. She ran her fingers through the toy's mane and tail and the strands of acrylic parted like water. It was, as the seller had promised, pristine.

Only now did Mary give herself over to truly admiring her new pony. Its marbled surface had a shiny, metallic sheen to it–twining rivulets of pink and red that shifted as Mary moved the figure back and forth in the light. A spray of green and gold stars freckled the pony's flank.

On top of the pony's head sprouted three yellow antennae of hard plastic–two topped with 3D stars and one with a tiny crescent moon. It's just like the promotional art Mary marvelled. Well, almost.

Mary reached into her drawer of pony brochures, pamphlets and other ephemera and withdrew the art card signed by (swoon!) Bonnie Zacherle herself. The glossy, 5 x 7 art card featured an image of four little ponies frolicking in space–a galaxy of stars spiralling behind them. Mary studied the image carefully, glancing up a few times to compare it to the pony in her hand. Her pony looked just like one of the four pictured... except where her pony's pink body was marbled with deep, crimson red, the pony in the artwork was swirled in a pearlescent pink, a few shades paler than her base body colour. Curious.

Otherwise satisfied with her visual and tactile inspection of her new treasure, Mary brought it up close to her nose to breathe in its factory-fresh fragrance. Her head immediately jerked back as a metallic scent assaulted her nostrils. This wasn't right. Where was that sweet, rubbery smell she knew so well? Hadn't the seller assured her this had come straight from a warehouse via a smoke and pet-free home?

Mary frowned down at the toy for some time before slowly lifting it back up close to her face. It looked fine. It felt fine. And yet... and yet...

Tentatively, Mary poked the very tip of her tongue out of her mouth and gingerly pressed it to the toy's plastic withers.

A taste like rust filled Mary's mouth, stinging her salivary glands. She pulled the toy away in disgust.

Could it be that the sheen of the pony's paint was made from real metal? This seemed unlikely to Mary. It must have been stored next to something when it was in the factory. Something metallic. The stench of the corroding material had leached into the porous plastic. Annoying, but it was nothing she could really blame the seller for.

"You're a stinky little thing!" Mary addressed the pony reproachfully, turning it to face her. "I'll have to keep you separate from the rest of the herd until you air out a bit."

Mary looked about the room for a suitable spot. Almost every surface in the room was already covered with ponies. Finally, her eyes alighted on the broad, bare windowsill. She hesitated. She didn't want such a rare and valuable pony to fade. Still, it would only be for a couple of days and the south-facing window got little light, anyway. Mary placed her new pony at the centre of the ledge, its display side facing the room, and stood back to look admiringly at the little pony whose crimson swirls glinted in the gloaming.

*

Mary overslept that night and when she finally awoke the following morning she had a hard time getting out of bed, feeling dazed and sluggish. Somehow she managed to drag herself through her morning routines and she was just about to head out to work when, passing by the pony room, something caught her eye.

Mary paused and retraced her steps back to stand in the doorway of the pony room, examining it with a frown. What was it that had caught her attention? She entered the room and scanned her shelves, but everything seemed to be in its place. Then she saw it. The new pony was no longer standing with its display side facing the room. Rather, it was turned to face the window.

Mary stalked into the room, bridling at the thought of someone tampering with her collection, but she pulled herself up short. *Don't be stupid!* She chastised herself. *There's no one else here. You must just have forgotten that you turned her that way.*

"Either that, or you decided you wanted to watch the birds!" she joked aloud then laughed, but the laugh sounded high and thin to her ears. I really am tired, she thought as she turned the pony back to face the room and finally headed out the door.

That whole day at work Mary felt out of sorts–prickly and irritable. Although she had never been particularly attached to her co-workers, she was normally able to at least endure their presence. Not today. Today everyone was slow and stupid; their conversation inane and repetitive.

Michael dropped off some papers for Mary to review and she could barely focus on a word he said. *I could beat your face in,* Mary thought, and wondered at the thought. *I could smash my fist right into your smug smile and you wouldn't even see it coming.* Far from unsettling, she found the thought somehow soothing.

By the end of the day Mary was exhausted. She left work without bidding her co-workers farewell and caught her usual tram home. Every time another passenger jostled or bumped against her she would grind her teeth and clench her fist around the handrail. She wasn't sure exactly what was wrong. She was just certain that it was everyone else's fault.

Arriving home, Mary still felt tense from the day's frustrations. She went to make herself a cup of tea, unaware that she was muttering angrily the whole time.

Steaming cup of tea in hand, Mary headed to the pony room to unwind. As soon as she entered the room a wave of relief washed over her. She sighed as she sat down in her pink desk chair and, reaching across to the side table with her spare hand, retrieved her laptop.

Mary surfed the net aimlessly for a while, sipping intermittently at her earl grey. She decided to check her bank account to make sure she wasn't overdrawn after paying for Starswirl. She wasn't. In fact, it looked like the payment hadn't gone through at all. Confused, Mary checked her PayPal account. Sure enough, the $500 she had paid the seller had been refunded. There was no note to explain why. Mary chewed at her lip as she stared at the refund wondering, Who is "Pale_Rider", anyway?

*

Mary didn't expect to find much when she looked Pale_Rider up on the forum, and that's exactly what she found. No threads. No posts. No sign whatsoever that the user even existed apart from the private messages she had sent to Mary and a profile page that was blank but for the username and the date she had signed up.

Mary was about to close the page when she decided to try one last thing. She opened the forum and typed "Pale_Rider" into the search field. One result was returned–a thread from two years ago titled "Who is Pale_Rider?".

Mary opened the thread:

MonsterIceCream:
Feb 12, 2017

Hi guys! I know I don't post here very often, but I received a weird message

from another user and I'm having trouble getting back in contact with her. I was hoping someone around here might know more about her?
Her username is Pale_Rider and she claims to have a Fancy Swirl prototype for sale, but she's not responding to any of my messages. Anyone know how I can get in touch with her?

-

my little pony collector:
Feb 12, 2017

I know a "Wave_Rider" but not a "Pale_Rider". Also, I thought the Fancy Swirls were never actually made? Sounds kind of shifty to me.

-

Evilbunnyfoofoo:
Feb 12, 2017

There's an account for Pale_Rider, but they haven't posted anything in the trading post. I agree with my little pony collector. Sounds like someone's just yanking your chain.

Mary scrolled past several posts. All expressing scepticism at the offer that had been made to MonsterIceCream, but none were able to throw any light on the identity of Pale_Rider.

A couple of months after the original post, MonsterIceCream posted again with an update:

MonsterIceCream:
Apr 21, 2017

Long-time no write! I finally got a message back from Pale_Rider and I decided to buy the pony from her. It arrived today and, although I couldn't say for sure if it's genuine or some sort of custom, it's definitely beautiful. I can't get a good photo of it in this light, so I'll have to wait till tomorrow to upload pictures.
Essentially it looks just like the pony in the Fancy Swirl promotional art—the one with the storm cloud cutie mark (Pale_Rider called it Swirlabout)—but instead of lilac the marbling on the body is a very pale silver. It looks white in most light.
There is just one teeny thing... the pony reeks! It smells like someone's dog buried it. It's otherwise in perfect

condition, though, so I don't know what's up with the smell.

Several users had responded to MonsterIceCream's update congratulating her on her purchase and asking to see pictures. A few commented that they still didn't believe it was genuine and some even suggested that MonsterIceCream herself was lying. The matter was never resolved though as, after that point, the thread just seemed to die. MonsterIceCream never posted any pictures of Swirlabout, nor did she respond to her accusers.

Lost in thought, Mary chewed absently at her lower lip. This was all too close for comfort. After staring at the abandoned thread for some time, Mary clicked on MonsterIceCream's username. The profile popped up. Scrolling through the user's activity Mary found that MonsterIceCream had started one last thread after the discussion about Pale_ Rider, this time in the "Wanted to Sell" section of the forum:

G1 Collection Free to Good Home
MonsterIceCream:
March 5, 2017

Hi guys. I need to get rid of my collection

and fast, so if you're a bargain hunter this is a great opportunity.
I have approximately 176 G1 ponies, most in very good to minty condition. Highlights include TE Mimic, Rapunzel with original barrettes and a prototype (or custom?) Swirlabout.
I don't have photos, but if you claim it now I'll send the whole lot to you for the price of postage.

-

Gingerbread:
March 5, 2017

I've just sent you a DM. Is this for real? Is something wrong?

-

MonsterIceCream:
March 6, 2017

Ever since I got Swirlabout I've started to feel differently about my collection. I know this sounds crazy, but they've started to creep me out. I can't handle all those little eyes staring at me all *the time. I feel like they're watching*

me. And the smell! My whole room smells like rotten eggs.
I feel sick and I just feel like getting rid of the ponies will be a huge weight off my chest. I'd try to sell them individually, but I just want them all gone now.

-

MonsterIceCream:
March 7, 2017

Claimed! Thank you all for your interest and your concern. I feel much happier now.

-

MonsterIceCream:
June 17, 2017

And I looked, and beheld a pale horse: and his name that sat on him was Death, and Hell followed him.

Mary reread MonsterIceCream's thread several times. The woman sounded genuinely disturbed. Mary felt a little twinge whenever she got to the part about the ponies smelling wrong. Her own pony didn't smell like rotten eggs, of course. But still...

Swivelling her chair around, Mary faced Starswirl, which was still sitting on the windowsill and still facing the room. She scooted over to the toy and picked it up. After a moment's hesitation, she gave it another sniff.

There it was again–that strange, metallic scent. It hadn't faded at all since she put the pony out to air. It smells stronger than ever, Mary thought, although she knew this made no sense. She didn't pull the pony away as she had the first time. Instead, she took another deep breath, letting the sharp scent pierce her nostrils. There was something almost pleasing about the smell, she thought. Unfamiliar, true, but not entirely unpleasant. It was somehow fresh and invigorating. Mary stuck out her tongue and licked the length of Starswirl's back. Her mouth was flooded with a taste like dirty coins. She shuddered and bit reflexively at her bottom lip, her flesh breaking out in goose bumps.

*

Mary slept fitfully that night. She had strange dreams.

She dreamt of ponies—which was not unusual—but these ponies were wrong.

Her collection was in disarray. Instead of the orderly rainbow she had taken such care to curate the figures were all jumbled up. Mary was sitting on the floor of her pony room brushing out the tail of Bouquet, one of her favourites. With each stroke, the tail grew longer–the key feature of the Brush and Grow line, but it just kept going. Mary set aside the brush and used both hands to draw inch upon inch of hair from the little plastic pony until almost a whole metre had come out of its back end. There was a slight hitch in the tail and Mary thought it must be about to stop, but instead there was a wet pop and she found herself pulling out a long, slimy trail of intestines.

Gasping, Mary tossed Bouquet aside in disgust. She tried to get to her feet, but the ground was pulsing and she couldn't steady herself. She spun around and braced herself against one of her pony shelves, and as she did so came face to face with her collection of Beddy-Bye Eye baby ponies. They each winked at her from weeping eyes that gazed out from raw and swollen sockets. Mary reeled back. The whole room spun and she caught glimpses of the rest of her collection–all hideously transformed.

Sweetheart Sisters teetered on legs so long and thin they looked ready to snap. The Sweetie Babies had their lips curled back to reveal large, rotten teeth in mottled gums. A rotten miasma wafted off the Perfume Puff ponies.

Undercutting all this was a rusty, metallic smell. Mary gazed up at the top of the shelf and saw Starswirl looming there over her. She was not changed like the others, and somehow that was more terrifying, for it was only then that Mary noticed the red pattern that covered Starswirl's body looked exactly like a network of veins. Mary tried to cry out but started to cough and gag as the smell grew stronger and threatened to overwhelm her.

*

Mary awoke with a start. Although it was a cool night, she found herself drenched in sweat. She mopped at her brow with her sleeve.

The dream was fresh in her mind. She could still see her beloved herd, all mutated and corrupted. She could still smell that pervasive metallic tang in the air.

Mary sat up. She really could smell it. The odour was overpowering. What's more, Mary finally recognised it for what it was.

On shaky legs she made her way down the corridor through the dark. With every step she took towards her pony room the scent grew stronger. When she reached the room, she hesitated for several heartbeats before flicking on the light.

In the sallow light Mary saw her collection in disarray, just as it had been in her dream. Ponies were scattered, apparently at random, over every surface in the room.

Right on top of her central pony shelf stood Starswirl, presiding over the havoc below. The red markings that marbled her body seemed to swirl and throb as Mary watched. Gazing up at the pony, Mary bit her lip so hard her mouth began to fill with blood, the taste metallic on her tongue.

NEARLY-PEOPLE

MELISSA FELT TRAPPED — trapped in the car with her family, trapped in this move she had resisted from the outset and trapped to a future she could only dread as terminally boring.

Passing through yet another dreary rural town, still several hours or so from their destination, Melissa and her family passed an antiques and collectables store with a vintage gumball machine and a child sized Noddy figure set out the front. "Ooooh, Dave, let's pull over!" her mother had pleaded. Melissa rolled her eyes. Antique stores were her mother's greatest weakness. Her father's greatest weakness, on the other hand, was her mother, so naturally they stopped.

Melissa flicked listlessly through a rack of vintage clothes (all miles too big) while her mother swooned over some moulded plastic lamp.

Her sister, Katie, ran past in a blur with a piercing squeal, some kind of antique rag-doll in an off-white dress clutched to her chest. When Katie reached their parents, she was red-faced and practically hyperventilating with excitement.

Melissa couldn't see what the fuss was all about. The doll was ugly. It looked like one of those Amish dolls she had seen in her 'Religions of the World' textbook, the ones that had no faces so as not to instil vanity in the hearts of little Amish children. It was bald, too, and lumpy, and its dress had a dark blotch that Melissa hoped was a tea stain.

But Katie wanted it. She wanted it with the furious intensity characteristic of a young child. She wanted it so badly her whole face purpled, threatening tears. Rather than face hours in a car trapped with a screaming, bawling child, Melissa's parents relented and bought her the doll.

When they went to pay, the elderly woman behind the counter commented, "I think this doll has been here longer than I have!"

"You'll be sad to see it go, then." Melissa's mother returned merrily. The old woman pursed her lips but said nothing.

*

"And here it is!" Melissa's father declared proudly as their car cruised past the sign reading 'Welcome to Baban'.

"It's lovely!" responded Melissa's mother. A little premature, Melissa thought, given they had just barely entered the town's outskirts.

"Isn't it lovely, girls?" her mother pressed, craning her neck to face the backseat where Melissa and Katie sat. Katie was too absorbed with her new doll to pay any attention to the outside world and Melissa, though she had heard her mother, continued to stare out the window in stony silence.

Melissa had made no secret of

the fact that she was unhappy about the move. At 15 years old, the prospect of leaving her school and friends to move halfway across the country to some tiny town she'd never heard of was a grim one indeed.

There had been tears on Melissa's last day at school, with hugs and solemn promises to stay in touch, but Melissa knew better. Some of her friends may send her a message or two at first, but soon enough the tyranny of distance would overwhelm the once solid friendships. There would be too many missed milestones, too many unshared day-to-day experiences, and so the friends would grow distant. She'd seen it happen before. This was not the first time her family had moved.

Melissa's mother tried again, her urgent enthusiasm verging on desperation, "Things will be different here. We can all start fresh! It will be like a new life..."

In the awkward silence that followed, Melissa continued to brood. Why did they have to move *here* of all places? What kind of town was so small it didn't even have its own cinema? The locals even dressed like hicks, Melissa observed as they drove down the optimistically named 'Main Street'. Outside a small florist Melissa could make out a figure who was actually wearing denim overalls, a flannel shirt and a large, daggy sun hat.

Melissa scoffed quietly and prepared to shoot the fashion victim a withering look as soon as the car came near enough.

Melissa leant into the window to meet the figure's eye she suddenly recoiled. "What is it?"

Her father chuckled, "I thought you'd like that. Those are the 'nearly-people'."

"*Nearly-people*?" Melissa said incredulously, drawing each word out in an effort to convey to her family the ridiculousness of the phrase.

"Yup!" her father continued brightly, "The tradition dates almost all the way back to the town's founding. Local businesses put them out front to bring good luck. There's one out the front of your school, too. There's some story behind that one. I think it must have been the first nearly-person."

Melissa was looking out the window again, taking note now of the numerous stationery figures–halfway between scarecrow and mannequin–

that dotted the main strip of shops. Each of them seemed to be dressed in the theme of their corresponding business. The nearly-person outside the bakery wore a chef's toque and black and white checked pants. Outside the post office was a dummy mailman with a large, canvas satchel. The one outside the lingerie store was modestly dressed in a blue dressing-gown and fluffy slippers. There was an almost startling array of the figures, all unique in style of dress and pose, but alike in one respect.

"Why don't they have any faces?" Melissa asked as they passed yet another mannequin–its blank head of hessian sacking a perfect void.

"It's always been that way." her father replied dismissively, "Aren't they neat?"

Melissa scoffed again. She did not think they were 'neat'. At best they were some twee rural custom. Something out of one of her mother's 'Country Living' magazines. At worst...

"Creepy." Melissa muttered under her breath.

By this stage Katie was looking out the window, too, a smile spreading across her pudgy face, "Look, Sally!"

she squealed, pressing her doll against the glass "They look like you!"

*

The house was much bigger than their old one, which Melissa had to admit was some consolation.

Her room was huge. It even had a bay window. True, the view included the gates of the local high school–not the most convivial of sights–but Melissa did not expect complete perfection.

At least she wouldn't have to share a room with Katie. She loved her sister, of course, but she could be a little brat sometimes and, besides, Melissa wanted some place that would be private. Some place that was just hers.

No sooner had she thought this than she looked up to see Katie standing in her doorway clutching her doll and watching in that curiously intent way that always made her uncomfortable.

"...Yes?" Melissa addressed Katie irritably.

"Sally doesn't like our new room. Can we trade?"

Melissa laughed. Her new room was almost twice the size of Katie's. "Nice try, squirt, but it's not happening."

Katie frowned. She lingered in the doorway for some time, glancing around the room, "Sally says this should be her room."

"Sally," responded Melissa through gritted teeth, "Can't say anything. Sally doesn't even have a mouth. Or eyes. She can't see the room. She can't even see *this*–" and with that Melissa sprung towards the doorway, ripped the doll out of Katie's grasp and flung it right down the hallway.

Katie stood stunned for a minute, then ran after her doll, screaming all the way. Melissa slammed the door shut behind her.

*

The school did indeed have its own nearly-person, just outside the front gates and dressed in the school uniform. She was taller and larger than the other nearly-people, but not inconceivably so. Maybe about a foot taller. If she were real, you'd call her a giant... though probably not to her face. As Melissa entered the schoolgrounds for the first time, she noticed that several of the students, the girls specifically, would touch the hem of the nearly-person's skirt as they passed through the entrance, appearing to mutter something as they did so.

School was every bit as depressing as Melissa had expected. The teachers were all old and stern and joyless. The other students were weirdly passive. As Melissa was brought before the class to introduce herself, her peers, all dressed identically in their school uniforms, gazed at her mildly. *They look exactly like cattle* Melissa thought with disdain. *I can't even tell one face from another.*

Arriving home that evening Melissa found her mother sitting on the armchair in the lounge-room, frowning.

"Hi Mum!" Melissa called as she flung her backpack onto the dining room table. "Oh, hello dear." replied her mother, looking up only briefly before returning her worried gaze to her lap.

"Is everything okay?" Melissa asked.

Her mother heaved a great sigh, then looked up to face her, "It's just Katie. She made such a fuss today about her doll needing eyes and a mouth and I said I would fix it, but it's just not turning out right."

"Let me see." urged Melissa, and her mother lifted Sally off her lap, turning it to face Melissa. Melissa grimaced, "What is that?" she asked, pointing at a black oblong stitched on to the lower part of the doll's face.

"That's her mouth!" snapped her mother, "I tried to make a smile, but it didn't look right so I filled it in."

"And why are the eyes black?"

"I only had black thread. Why? What colour should they be?"

Melissa had no answer. All she knew is that the black embroidered eyes looked like gaping, empty sockets. The pair returned to staring at the doll critically.

"I know!" Melissa's mother cried triumphantly and began rummaging around in her sewing basket before retrieving two white buttons. She sewed one each of these into the black circles on Sally's face. "There!"

"... Yeah," said Melissa uncertainly, "Much better."

Whatever Melissa thought of her mother's 'improvements' to the doll, Katie was delighted. She swept Sally up in her arms and spun around in circles in the lounge-room. "See!" she cried as she came to a shaky stop in front of Melissa, “Sally’s a real person now!”

Melissa looked down at the doll with its broad mouth and sewn-on eyes. “Sure, squirt. Whatever you say.”

*

Over time Melissa did make a few friends among her classmates–girls who were perhaps a little bolder, a little more animated than the rest. There wasn’t anywhere interesting to hang out in Baban. On weeknights they would hang out at the skate-park and watch with an air of calculated indifference as kids in baggy t-shirts performed jumps and tricks on the concrete slopes.

Most Friday nights they ended up at the 24-hour McDonald’s down the end of Main Street. A pair of old sneakers flung over a nearby powerline hinted that there was more to be procured there than thickshakes and McNuggets, but Melissa wasn’t that bored, not yet.

One Friday evening, having had their fill of the fluorescent lighting and plastic seating offered by McDonalds, the three friends were slowly wending their way back down Main Street. Sarah was talking in breathy tones about her latest crush, Dean. Or was it Scott? Or Shaun? They were all the same to Melissa.

Gradually, her friend's voice started to grate on Melissa. The soppiness of her unrequited affection was childish. Pathetic. All at once Melissa bounded up to one of the nearly-people (the old-fashioned news-boy out the front of the local paper), flung her arms around its shoulders and sighed, "Oh, Dean! Touch me! Hold me!" then began to cackle with laughter. Her friends did not join her.

"You shouldn't do that." said Sarah. She didn't sound hurt or angry. She sounded scared.

"What?" queried Melissa, still clinging amorously to the figure.

"It's not...respectful." Sarah replied.

"Respectful?" Melissa scoffed. She rapped at the nearly-person's head with her knuckle. Irene winced as it she had been struck. "It's just a dummy!"

"They've been here forever." Sarah explained in a patronising tone that made Melissa's hackles rise, "No one knows how long. No one knows who made them. When a business changes hands the new owners dress up the nearly-people, but otherwise no one touches them. They're, like, cursed or something."

Melissa laughed, but found herself withdrawing her arms from the mannequin.

"Chris Murphy stole a hat from one once, and the next day his parents were in a terrible car crash. And my Mum says when she was little another kid used to mess around with them and he went missing. They never found him."

Melissa sneered, "What is it going to do? Give me the evil eye?" She waved a hand in front of the nearly-person's blank face.

"They used to paint faces on them." Irene piped up and both Melissa and Sarah turned to face her, "My Nonna says so. Eyes. Mouths. It was supposed to make them look friendly for tourists, but locals started complaining. The eyes would follow you down the street, they said. And then there were the whispers. Nonna says on some nights, even when she was home in bed, she could hear them talking to each other"

"...What happened then?" asked Melissa. Irene shrugged, "The paint eventually wore off in the weather. They decided not to paint them again."

The three girls considered this in silence for a few moments, then Sarah insisted, "You're not supposed to touch them."

"What about the one at school?" Melissa retorted, "You touch it every day. I've seen you!"

"You mean Mother?" asked Irene, "That's different. That's traditional."

"I'm sorry, did you just call that dummy mother?" said Melissa incredulously, then turned to Sarah, ready to laugh, but Sarah just nodded her head, "That's what she's called! Back when the school used to be a convent, people called her 'mother' because she was supposed to represent the virgin Mary. If you touch her every school day, it's supposed to guarantee your place in heaven or something."

"That's not quite right." Irene frowned, "It's from back when there was a maternity hospital on that site. People called her 'mother' because she was supposed to gather up the souls of all the stillborn babies and guide them safely to heaven. If you touch her every day, it's supposed to mean you'll never have a baby die in childbirth."

Melissa froze and was grateful for the gloom that hid the sudden flush of her cheeks. "Hmm," she offered, then, standing on her tip-toes, leant in and kissed the news-boy nearly-person on what should have been its cheek. "Good night Deanie-weenie!" she pouted then, turning to her dumbstruck friends, "Come on. Let's go."

*

When Melissa got home her parents were already in bed. She headed to the lounge-room and as she entered, a faint flickering of lights told her the TV was already on. There was a soft murmuring that did not match the images on the screen. Melissa stood watching for a while as images of soldiers and blasts of gunfire played out, all in silence but for a soft, persistent whispering that undercut it all. Melissa felt uneasy until she noticed Katie curled up on the lounge with Sally propped upright on top her.

"Katie!" Melissa hissed. The whispers cut off and Katie sat up, rubbing at her eyes. "I was sleeping." she said accusingly.

"Yeah, and you were talking in your sleep, too."

"Wasn't!" pouted Katie, still rubbing at her face.

Melissa sighed. "Why aren't you in your room?" she asked.

"Sally doesn't like it in there." Katie replied. Melissa just rolled her eyes before turning off the TV and scooping up her sister in both arms to carry her back to her bedroom. Katie fell back asleep before Melissa had even tucked her under the covers.

Suddenly weary, Melissa returned to her own room and climbed into bed. As she drifted into sleep she fancied she could still hear Katie whispering to herself.

*

Melissa awoke with a strange feeling. Sitting up in bed she peered warily around the room until she saw Sally, sitting on Melissa's dressing table and facing the mirror as if admiring her own reflection.

Melissa let out a guttural yell, sprang out of bed and snatched up the doll before storming out of her room.

"Don't go in my room!" she

screamed as she entered the kitchen where Katie was eating a bowl of cereal.

"Sally!" Katie happily squealed with a mouth full of Coco-Pops. She reached out with both of her arms.

Melissa marched over and slammed the doll into the table, making Katie start. "Did you hear me, squirt? I said don't go into my room. Not ever!"

Katie picked up the doll and smoothed its ruffled dress. Without looking up at her sister she said simply, "Sally likes your room better."

"M-ummm!" Melissa screeched in her frustration.

"Katie, dear. Stay out of your sister's room," their mother said absently from the kitchen sink.

"Okay!" piped Katie.

She did not, however, keep to her word, as it seemed every day after that Melissa would wake to find Sally somewhere in her room–sometimes on the dressing table, sometimes at her desk and once even tucked beside her in bed. Most often, though, Melissa would find the doll sitting in the bay window facing out towards the school.

At first, these incidents made Melissa furious and she even asked her parents if she could put a lock on her bedroom door, but as the days wore into weeks she grew used to Sally's appearances. She even started guessing where the doll had been placed every morning.

"Where are you, Miss Sally?" she would ask with a yawn as she climbed out of bed "Did you sleep well last night? Get all of your beauty rest?"

Katie, on the other hand, grew bored with the doll, being less and less excited when Melissa returned it to her in the morning.

"What's the matter, squirt?" Melissa would ask "Don't you like Sally anymore?". Katie would shrug and drag the doll off to her own bedroom. Melissa. As the younger girl dragged her doll carelessly back to the room, letting its stuffed head butt against the doorframe, Melissa would wince involuntarily.

One day, rather than bringing the doll back to Katie, Melissa decided to leave Sally sitting in the bay window. She looked so comfortable, after all, propped up by several cushions, the skirt of her dress fanned about her and her hands resting neatly in her lap. As Melissa left for school that morning, she looked back at her bedroom window and smiled as she saw Sally's button eyes gazing back at her.

*

At school that day Melissa found it even harder than usual to concentrate. She was looking out the window back towards her house wondering if Sally was still sitting in her window or if Katie had retrieved her, when there was the sudden slam of a wooden ruler against her desk almost causing her to jump out of her seat

"Miss Reed!" barked old Mrs Munter, the Humanities teacher. "If you could tear yourself away from the outside world for one minute, we were discussing the local history assignment. Now, I know you are new to town and may have trouble coming up with a topic, but—"

"What about Mother?" Melissa asked, surprising herself. Where had that thought come from?

The room was in absolute silence. Mrs Munter blinked down at Melissa a few times before responding with a quiet, "What?"

"I could write about 'Mother'." Melissa reiterated, "The nearly-person out the front of the school? I'm sure there are some interesting things to say about it. 'Her', I mean."

Silence again, except for one nervous titter from somewhere behind Melissa. Mrs Munter stared down vacantly at Melissa. She seemed just about to say something when the bell rang and the students all got out of their seats and rushed out the door. Melissa was about to join them when Mrs Munter raised a hand to stay her.

"I think, Miss Reed, that you'd best stay behind so we can discuss this proposal of yours."

As the last stragglers made their way out of the room, Melissa leant back in her chair and crossed her arms. She didn't relish the idea of being stuck here with Mrs Munter, but then she didn't mind missing out on some of her next class.

Mrs Munter stared down at Melissa, who couldn't help but marvel at the deep crevasses that marked the teacher's angular face. "She's practically a fossil," Melissa thought to herself, "How is she even upright?"

Finally, Mrs Munter spoke:

"I don't know who told you about Mother, but that story is very... sensitive to this town. I don't appreciate you making a joke out of it."

Melissa frowned.

"I wasn't trying to be funny. I just heard a few stories about the nearly-person and I thought it would make an interesting essay."

Mrs Munter eyed Melissa sceptically.

"Don't *you* think it's interesting?" asked Melissa, her tone slightly mocking, "After all, you must know all the stories."

From behind her glasses Mrs Munter's eyes seemed to glaze. She glanced up from Melissa to look out the window and in a surprisingly soft voice spoke, "When I was young, my grandmother told a story about a local woman whose baby girl went missing. This must have happened years ago, back when the town was not much more than a small collection of farms and a church. The woman never recovered from her grief. Went quite mad with it, some said. As the years went on, she started to make the girls of the town, the ones who were about the age her daughter would have been, quite uncomfortable. She wouldn't stalk them, as such, just watch them intently whenever they passed.

The girls grew to be quite scared of her. Rumours started spreading around that the woman was planning to abduct girls to replace her own missing child. No one knew what to do about the rumours. Most people in the town felt sorry for the woman. I'm not quite sure how it first started, but as a kind of talisman the teenage girls in town would touch the largest of the nearly-people and address it as 'Mother'. Some said that the woman would leave girls alone if she thought they belonged to the nearly-person. Others said the nearly-person itself would protect any girls who declared themselves its daughter. Whatever the reasoning behind it, it grew into a tradition. Some people say that when the woman died her soul was transferred into the nearly-person so that she could be mother to all the girls in town."

Here, Mrs Munter's voice trailed off, then all at once her attention snapped back to Melissa and her voice was as crisp as usual, her beady eyes as sharp.

"You wouldn't understand,

Melissa. You're not local. And you're not a mother."

*

When Melissa got home, she went straight to her bedroom and sat in the bay window facing the school. She pulled Sally onto her lap and absently stroked at the doll's bald head as she gazed at Mother's silhouette, just barely discernible at this distance.

For reasons she did not understand it bothered Melissa that there were so many different stories behind the giant nearly-person. "How can it be," Melissa thought to herself "That everyone calls her 'Mother', but no one seems to agree on why?"

There was something else that was troubling her, too. Something that Mrs Munter had said:

"You're not local. And you're not a mother."

Still staring out the window, Melissa gripped Sally tightly in her hands, her fingertips digging into the doll's lumpy body.

She had tried not to think of it, the 'other' reason her family had to move.

Drawing Sally up to her chest with one arm she ran her free hand under her school skirt along her lower abdomen, as if searching for some sign there of what had happened inside her, some tell-tale scar. All she felt was smooth skin over soft flesh. That night Melissa took Sally to bed with her.

*

In the morning Sally wasn't there. Melissa threw back her bedding to see if she had kicked Sally further down into bed as she slept, but the bed was empty.

Melissa looked up in confusion and that is when she saw Sally, once more sitting in the bay window.

Up until now it had been easy for Melissa to believe Katie had been sneaking into her room in the middle of the night. It had been *necessary* for her to believe it. But now... Surely Katie could not have retrieved the doll from Melissa's grasp without waking her?

Slowly, Melissa approached the window "Sally?" she called cautiously as she reached out to touch the doll. Melissa thought she heard a sigh, soft and sad, though it could have just come from herself. She turned to look out in the direction Sally was facing and saw the school, abandoned on that dreary Saturday morning but for the ubiquitous presence of Mother propped up beside the front gates.

That day, Melissa carried Sally around with her as she hung about the house. Melissa cradled Sally as she ate her breakfast, she rocked Sally as she picked out her wardrobe for the day, she sat with Sally on her knee as she blankly watched TV, and all the while she had a vague, drawn look on her face. No one questioned her. Katie had evidently lost all interest in the doll and their parents were either too embarrassed or too afraid to call attention to the behaviour, although they exchanged concerned looks with each other and would whisper about it when they were in bed that night.

Melissa didn't care. Behind her vacant stare her thoughts were crystallising and an idea was forming.

Late that afternoon Melissa told her parents she was going to catch up with Irene. She went to her room and surreptitiously tucked Sally into her backpack before heading off on her bike in the direction of the school.

Out the front of the empty schoolgrounds Melissa spent quite some time staring up at the towering figure of Mother clad in her familiar school uniform. Eventually, Melissa spoke.

"I guess we have that one thing in common," she said half grudgingly, half wistfully. "We both lost something." She stood there in silence as though awaiting a response, then scoffed at herself. She bent down and retrieved Sally from her backpack. She stroked the doll's hideous face lovingly, then gently placed it in Mother's outspread arms.

Melissa waited. Nothing happened. She frowned. She was not sure what she had expected. Just something. Just as Melissa was feeling her most ridiculous, the setting sun sent a ray of red-orange light glaring over the horizon. It hit Mother's back and the nearly-person and doll were haloed in a rich, warm glow. They were the perfect tableaux of mother and child and as Melissa gazed up at them in wonder she felt light, as if something that had been weighing on her had finally lifted and she could, for the first time in a long time, breathe again.

The effect lasted only a few

moments before the sun set and the lighting changed. A bitter wind approached from the East and Sally fell out of Mother's arms and into the mud at the nearly-person's feet. Melissa promptly scooped the doll up, shoved it without ceremony back into her bag, then climbed on her bike to head home.

*

Once home, Melissa lifted the lid of the rubbish bin and prepared to toss Sally in, but something stayed her. There was something about those button eyes with their black, embroidered sclerae; something about that gaping, toothless mouth. The doll was just an empty vessel now, she told herself, just a pile of poorly sewn-together rags... and yet...

Pulling Sally back to her chest, Melissa slammed the bin closed. After a moment's hesitation she flung open the recycling bin instead and rummaged through its contents until she found the box from her new pair of Nikes. She lay Sally gently, almost tenderly, in the box, pulling the tissue paper over the doll's face so that it covered her like a veil.

Or a shroud.

She would bury the box in the back garden. Somewhere nice. Beneath the grevillea, perhaps. When it came right down to it, Sally was a person, after all. Well, nearly.

NECROMANTIC

SILK BRIDE

Heather *WAS PLEASED* to find out that Justine was to wear silk to the wedding–an ivory shift pleated from the waist and accented with tiny seed pearls. Heather was surprised that her daughter had chosen something so traditional. She was, in fact, relieved that Justine had not chosen something in black, like the rest of her wardrobe.

"Perhaps she's maturing," Heather thought, still hoping that her adult daughter would grow out of 'the Goth thing'.

The news about the hen's night, however, was less encouraging.

"—Why can't you just have a nice kitchen tea? You like tea! We could use your great-grandmother's tea service and—"

"—Mum!" said Justine with a roll of her eyes, "Nobody does 'kitchen teas' anymore. None of my friends even know what a kitchen tea is! Nowadays the bridesmaids tailor the hen's night to suit the bride's interests. People do life-drawing classes or wine tastings or —"

"But, a haunted house!?" Heather spluttered, still incredulous.

Justine sighed and tried to keep her tone even as she explained: "Wilma put a lot of thought into these plans, and I think it's sweet..." Heather scoffed at this, but Justine continued "...Besides, it's not as if it's a real haunted house! It's just Wilma's grandmother's old place. She's off on another cruise and is letting us use the house while she's away."

"The invite says 'haunted house'" Heather pressed, waving the gilt-edged card in her daughter's face.

"It's just a theme, Mum. It will be fun! We'll all get dressed up and we'll sit around and tell ghost stories and stuff, like when I was a kid."

"Well don't expect me to get involved in all that," huffed Heather.

"Mum, you have to be there," insisted Justine, "After all, you're the mother of the bride."

*

"Are you sure this is the right address?" asked Heather, for what must have been the dozenth time. "It really doesn't look like anybody is home."

She had a point. The house, an elegant Victorian building that must have surely looked pretty by the light of day had a grim and imposing attitude that dismal, starless night. Not to mention there was not a single light visible on the property.

"Of course it's the right address!" Justine insisted, before peering at the invite again in the dim light.

The pair stood indecisively on the doorstep for a few moments longer, before Heather eventually pushed past her daughter to reach for the doorknocker. It was large and shaped roughly like a star and... it *moved.* Heather squealed and snatched her hand back as the huntsman spider that had been sitting right in the middle of the door quickly crawled up onto the door frame.

Justine could not suppress a giggle.

“I don't see what's so funny!” snapped Heather.

“Mu-um!” exclaimed Justine, still smiling “It's just a huntsman. They're completely harmless! In fact, they eat pests, so really they're helpful to have around.”

Heather eyed the top of the door frame sceptically.

Justine placed her hands on her mother's shoulders and gently moved the woman aside before knocking on the great oak-panelled door. Almost immediately the handle turned and the door slowly creaked open to reveal a tall, broad-shouldered young woman in a white evening gown holding aloft an ornate candelabra.

“More victims!” she declared in velvet-rich tones.

“Will!” Justine cried then, laughing, leapt forward to embrace her friend, careful to avoid the wax that dripped from the lit tapers.

"Hello, bride-to-be!" Wilma returned. "Hello, Mrs Buckley!"

"Good evening, Wilma," Heather responded a little stiffly "What's wrong with the lights?"

Grinning, Wilma beckoned for the two women to follow her inside, explaining as they progressed "We turned the power off at the fuse-box. It was Mandy's idea. Really adds to the spooky vibe, don't you think?"

Candles were scattered all around the entryway and down the front hallway, lighting a flickering path toward the lounge-room. Entering, they gasped. Every surface was littered with candles of different sizes and shapes, tiny flames dancing in the gloom.

"It's beautiful" Justine sighed and Heather, impressed despite herself, commented, "It's like being inside a church!"

"Thank goodness it's not a church," said Wilma. "Or I might just burst into flames." Justine snickered. Heather pursed her lips but made no comment.

Mandy, Wilma's younger sister, was sitting on a pink, suede sofa in the middle of the room, a drink already in hand. She rose when she saw Justine and Heather, a look of relief on her face. Sitting at the other end of the sofa, legs folded up neatly beneath her, was Justine's other bridesmaid, Anna.

"The gang's all here!" chirped Anna, sweeping her blonde hair back behind her ears and adjusting her glasses fastidiously "I guess that means we can start the tour."

For the better part of an hour Wilma led the small party on an extensive and creative tour of the substantial property. They started at the top of the house, skipping the attic (it was locked) and made their way gradually down. For every room they entered or objet d'art they passed Wilma had a different chilling tale to tell. She told of eerie hauntings, bloody murders and demonic possessions–her stories becoming gradually more lurid and vile as the tour progressed until they bordered on the ludicrous.

As Wilma finished spinning a story of a young woman who fell in love with a ghost and was just about to lead them all into a large bedroom she dubbed 'the room of echoes', Justine reached over and squeezed her mother's hand reassuringly.

"See," she told her. "It's not really haunted at all."

"Oh, but it is!" insisted Mandy, her eyes bright even in the gloom. She turned eagerly to her sister, "Tell them, Will."

Wilma quietly went and sat on the edge of one of two single-beds in the room. She paused for effect—readjusting her dress and positioning the candelabra so that it cast dramatic shadows on her face—and then began, "It all happened in this very room...

"When we were little, our mother would sometimes send us to stay with Nana. Nana was always strict, but she'd still do the usual grandma things–tell us stories, feed us too many sweets. At night she would tuck us in to bed, right here," she patted at the mattress "Before heading off to her own room to say her evening prayers.

"When we got a little older–about six and eight–we decided we would stay up late to tell stories. We waited until the light went off in Nana's room and we knew she had gone to sleep, then we began whispering to each other. This became our new ritual until one night, almost an hour after Nana's light went out, we heard a scraping sound coming from somewhere above our room. It was like someone dragging something heavy along the floorboards. The sound went on for minutes and then stopped abruptly. Then, after a pause there was this frantic, scurrying noise. It was like masses of people were running back and forth throughout the room, their shoes tapping on the floorboards–"

"–As if Nana would let anyone wear shoes in the house!" scoffed Mandy.

Wilma cleared her throat meaningfully. "Anyway, the scurrying went on for some time until it gradually petered out. In the silence that followed we lay there, frozen in terror. We did not sleep that night."

"There must have been some explanation for it," commented Anna. "Did you say anything to your Nana?"

Wilma nodded her head gravely, "Over Fruit Loops the next morning I told her everything about what we had heard..."

"...And?" prompted Justine. "What did she do?"

"The same thing she always does," Mandy chimed in. "Told us we were being stupid and gave us another serve of food."

"But, did anything like that ever happen again?" Justine pressed.

Wilma spoke again, "After that night we gave up the idea of staying up late to talk. Before bed we would have a hot mug of Milo and then try to fall asleep as soon as possible.

"Still, on some visits if one or the other of us couldn't get to sleep we would hear it again–the scraping and the scurrying. But we never both heard it on the same night and, as we got into our teens, neither of us heard it ever again."

For several seconds no one spoke, until Anna's grating tones finally cut through the silence, "It was probably possums."

"Think what you like!" snapped Wilma "All I know is that there's something not quite right about this place." She stood up and strode towards the door, beckoning the others to follow. "It's time we entered the last room on this floor, and the most terrifying stop on our tour—the dragon's lair!"

When they entered the room Justine's first impression was of an old-fashioned chocolate box—all pink satin and ruffles. Every surface was cluttered with twee knick-knacks—curly-haired shepherdesses, droopy-eyed children and a host of cutesy angels. It was, of course, the bedroom of Wilma and Mandy's grandmother.

Justine shuddered as she inspected a shelf of ceramic clowns: "I can see why you said it was scary."

"Creepy," agreed Anna.

Heather didn't approve of the girls' comments. She had an art graduate's appreciation for kitsch and, besides, it seemed unkind to be so critical of the elderly woman's most personal space, particularly when she had allowed them to make use of her home.

"How is Valerie?" Heather asked Wilma pointedly.

"Same as she always is," Mandy spoke before her sister had time to. "Sour!"

Suddenly, Justine gave a little squeal and the others all spun to face her. She was standing beside Valerie's bed, where she had discovered a white veil lying spread across the quilted doona.

Atop the veil, was a stiff piece of card upon which was written in cramped, spindly letters, the words, 'For the bride-to-be'.

Justine whisked the veil off the

bed and, as she did so, something fell to the polished floorboards with a clatter. Stooping down, Anna picked up a small wrought-iron key. She held it up for the others to see and, when she was met only with shrugs, she pocketed it.

Everyone returned their attention to the veil, which Justine hung delicately over her head. The veil was made of the finest lace-work–silken threads wound together in an ornate pattern of loops and whorls–so white it seemed to glow.

Heather reached out to stroke the material and was shocked by how light and insubstantial it was.

"It's like water," she sighed.

"I hate to be the one to say this," piped Anna (the others collectively groaned) "But it doesn't match your dress."

Justine's face fell. She slid the veil off and examined it again.

"Oh, what a pity!" cried Heather.

Justine shrugged, then draped the veil over her mother's head, announcing,

"Just for tonight, you can be a bride again."

The veil clung to Heather's hair as sturdily as if it was fastened with pins. Slowly, Heather approached the antique vanity mirror in the corner of the room to view her reflection. The veil framed her face and trailed down past her shoulders—a diaphanous cascade of spun sugar. Heather wasn't sure whether it was the veil itself or the flattering effect of the candlelight, but the face that gazed back at her from the mirror was almost unrecognisable to her–pretty and fresh. She could not suppress a little smile as she admired her own radiance.

"...And that concludes our chilling tour!" proclaimed Wilma with a ghoulish cackle. "Now if you'll all follow me back to the kitchen, I think it's time we had some more refreshments before we start on the next activity."

The kitchen was large and tidy, with almost nothing on the bench-tops apart from an electric kettle. The deep, Belfast sink had been filled with ice and Mandy fished around in it for a bit before withdrawing two beer bottles. She proffered one to Heather, who demurred, then handed it to Justine before cracking the other open herself and taking several deep swigs.

Heather slowly wandered through the kitchen, running her hands over the cool, marble bench-tops and admiring the neat, open design of the space. She had heard the girls say that Valerie had, when she was younger, been an accomplished cook and she could believe that this kitchen would be a joy to work in. She could imagine Valerie bustling about happily in it. Dreamily, Heather reached up and opened one of the cabinets.

A shower of dust rained down on Heather and she swatted at it, blinking and spluttering.

Justine rushed over. "Mum!" she cried. As she approached the glow of her candle revealed that the 'dust' that had fallen in Heather's face was actually a teaming mass of tiny spiders.

Heather shrieked and waved her hands all the more frantically, virtually slapping herself in the face.

"It's okay, it's okay!" Justine tried to reassure her, reaching up to delicately remove a spider that was clinging to the edge of Heather's veil. "They're just little money spiders. They're good luck!" Smiling, she watched the spider as it wandered along the length of her finger, then gently lowered it to the bench-top, where it quickly scuttled out of sight.

"...Nana always calls them 'sheet weavers,'" Wilma commented.

"Actually," Anna cut in "Their proper name is 'Linyphiidae'."

Meanwhile, Mandy took the final sip of her beer then cracked open a fresh bottle. "Will you be having that drink now, Mrs Buckley?" she asked archly. Heather, still trembling, took a few deep breaths before she responded,

"Thank you, Mandy. A red wine would be lovely."

Once they all had a drink (or, in Mandy's case, three) in hand they retired to the lounge-room, where Wilma encouraged everyone to join her sitting on her grandmother's mohair rug. She clapped her hands together decisively, "Alright! Next up for this evening, and not for the faint of heart, we are going to practice the ancient and mysterious art of necromancy."

Justine let out an appreciative, "Ooh!"

Heather set her lips.

"To do so, we are going to use, this–" Wilma reached into a large leather satchel that lay beside her and pulled out a flat piece of plywood "– a Ouija board!"

"Actually," Anna interjected "I

think you'll find it's pronounced 'oui', like the French and 'ja', like the German."

"So it's a 'yes-yes' board?" asked Justine.

"Essentially!" Anna responded with a smirk.

Mandy rolled her eyes and took another swig of her beer. Wilma continued, "Anyway... whatever you want to call it, tonight it's our window to the other side." She ran her perfectly manicured hands slowly, almost lovingly, over the surface of the board.

"Where's the planchette?" asked Anna.

"A-ha!" cried Wilma, "It's right..." she rummaged through the satchel, her smooth features gradually giving way to a frown.

"You forgot it, didn't you?" crowed Mandy.

Wilma shot her a venomous look, "It's... fine" she said stiffly. Regaining her composure she added, "We just need a glass or something."

"It will have to be a bloody small glass!" Mandy said, tapping a fingernail at the tiny, closely spaced letters on the board. "I wonder if Nana has any shot glasses?" she added in a voice heavy with irony.

Wilma looked like she was about to snap at Mandy but, fortunately for once, Anna cut in.

"If you just need something with a window," she said. "We have this." And with that she retrieved the small iron key from her pocket and handed it to Wilma.

The key was solid, but small enough so as not to be too heavy. The head was wrought into a series of circles and ovals, with the centre oval being just large enough to view the board's letters through.

"Perfect!" cried Wilma, "Now, let's begin."

There followed quite a bit of preamble where Wilma, in typically dramatic fashion, warned of the dangers inherent in interacting with the spirit world, called for protection from evil and malicious forces and, finally, invoked any spirits present to make themselves known.

The party started with their hands linked together in a ring and then, when Wilma's dramatics were over, they each placed a finger (that was all that would fit) lightly on the key.

They each took turns asking questions of the board, all except

Heather who stubbornly refused to engage with the frivolity, although she kept her finger resolutely on the key. The questions ranged from the superficial to the metaphysical. The women, who with a free hand each were able to continue their drinking, asked about late relatives, deceased pets and long-dead celebrities and historical figures.

Throughout the proceedings the women pleaded and begged, taunted and jeered–anything to try and get a response to their questions–but the key remained stoutly in place. That is, until Wilma made one final plea,

"Are there any messages at all from the other side?"

The key twitched. As the party watched the key began to slowly slide around the surface of the board, pausing with the aperture over a succession of letters. Heather began to tremble slightly. Seeing her mother's discomfort, Justine chided, "Stop mucking around, Mandy!"

"It's not me!" insisted Mandy, although her voice was full of laughter.

"W-I-L-" Anna began to read out, gazing at the board with intense concentration.

"'Will'! It must be for you, sis!" squawked Mandy, but Wilma hissed at her to be quiet as Anna continued, "L-Y-O-U-M-A-R-".

"It must be Wilma moving it," muttered Mandy. "She's trying to get me in trouble". This time it was Heather who shushed the young woman. Leaning in now, her face flushed from the three glasses of pinot noir she had downed during the game, it seemed like Justine's mother was finally engaging with the evening's activities.

"R-Y-M-E-" Anna intoned solemnly.

The key came to a halt. There was a pause while the women arranged the letters in their heads and then a sudden explosion of laughter.

"Nice one, Mandy!" Justine said, though Mandy, through fits of giggles, continued to insist, "It wasn't me!"

Even Heather was smiling as she said to Justine, "Well, dear, aren't you going to answer?"

"Hmm..." Justine prevaricated "I'm not sure if I should. What would George think?"

Then, as though of one will, all five women, laughing, pushed the key decisively to the corner of the board marked 'Yes'.

*

While Wilma packed away the board, passing the key to Heather for safe-keeping, the others refreshed their drinks and settled into the plump cushions that were scattered across the lounge-room's sofa and armchairs. Anna had slipped away to use the 'lavatory', as she insisted upon calling it, and there was a general mellowing of the atmosphere, as though the evening were winding down.

Heather gazed over at Justine, who had her left hand raised to observe the way her white-gold-and-moonstone engagement ring glowed softly in the candlelight. Whether it was the congenial atmosphere in the room, the joy behind the purpose of their gathering or the effect of a full bottle of wine to herself, Heather felt a sudden rush of pride as she looked upon her daughter. Although they sometimes had their differences, in that moment Heather thought she would do anything for her little girl. Heather's reverie was interrupted when Wilma, standing up from the floor, addressed the room. “Hasn’t Anna been in the bathroom for quite a long time?”

Mandy pulled a face, “She probably got lost!” she scoffed. There followed a brief silence in which the women considered this possibility for, in truth, Anna was known for her poor sense of direction. It was Justine who eventually dismissed the suggestion.

“The house isn’t that big.” she insisted.

Wilma clapped her hands together, causing the three other women to start.

“I know!” she cried. “We’ll make a game of it! We’ll each go and search for Anna by ourselves. Whoever brings her back to the lounge-room, wins.”

“‘Wins what?” enquired Mandy suspiciously.

“Why, my eternal love and admiration!” answered Wilma.

Mandy slumped back into her chair, “Bor-ing!”

“Alright. How about the losers each pay the winner ten dollars?” suggested Wilma.

Settling on these terms, the women each took a candle holder and separated out to explore the darkened house alone.

*

Heather moved warily up the first flight of stairs, the meagre light of her candle enough to see the next two steps ahead of her but no more. Her convivial spirits had begun to cool almost immediately after she split up from Justine and the others and now she was left with a feeling of abandonment and the beginnings of a headache.

With her free hand she clung to the bannister as she gradually inched her way upstairs. She was frightened, and that made her angry. "Silly girls!" she thought to herself, "Aren't they too old for hide-and-seek?"

When she reached the top of the stairs Heather paused. She didn't know her way around the unfamiliar house, especially in the dark, and she was unsure where to go next. She peered into her shadowy surroundings and tried to remember where Wilma had led them on their tour.

Now, how did it go? First there was the torture chamber, then the bloody room. Past that was the mirrored hall and then... that's right–the dragon's lair! Wasn't Valerie's bedroom somewhere just to the right of these stairs?

Waving one arm in front of herself to test for obstacles, Heather shuffled her way through the wide corridor until her searching hand hit the cold brass of a doorknob. With a sigh of relief, she turned the handle and entered Valerie's bedroom.

The room–pink and rosy–glowed in the candlelight. Heather went and sat on the bed. Her head was starting to swim now and she regretted every drop of wine she had drunk. Setting her candle on the bedside table, Heather closed her eyes, took in several deep breaths and waited for the room to stop spinning.

She felt a little better in this room than she had out in the hallway or on the stairs. The bed was soft and comfortable and the floral prints on the wall, assorted perfumes and toiletries at the dressing-table and pink, pink, pink everywhere gave the room an almost cheerful atmosphere. Heather smiled softly and, without meaning to, without even thinking about it, lay out on the bed, rested her cheek on a ruffled pillow and fell asleep.

*

When Heather first awoke she did not remember where she was and panic gripped her. When, after a few startled moments, she recognised her surroundings, her confusion gave way to another kind of uneasiness... for how long had she been asleep?

Heather sat bolt upright and immediately regretted it, clutching at her aching head. She felt as though something were scratching at the inside of her skull.

Scrape, scrape, scrape.

Gritting her teeth, Heather stood up and reached for the candle, realising to her dismay that it had almost burnt out. She would have to make her way back to the lounge-room, she decided. The girls would probably all be waiting there, wondering where she was. There would be light in the lounge-room, too.

With the stubby remnants of her candle in hand, Heather made her unsteady way out of the bedroom and back into the hallway. She was making her way towards the stairs when there came again that grating feeling–*scrape, scrape, scrape*. She realised now that the vibrations were coming not from her throbbing skull but, rather, from somewhere above her.

She raised her candle aloft and stared at the cracked, plaster ceiling, the thudding in her head now matched by the hammering of her heart. When the scraping stopped, Heather stood rooted to the spot for some time before she finally lowered the candle and resumed her progress down the hallway towards the stairs.

W*hy hadn't the girls come to find her?* Heather wondered to herself. Why hadn't they stopped their silly games and turned the power back on? She squinted into the darkness before her, trying to make out her way. Surely the stairs were just a couple of metres ahead of her now? Somewhere just to the left?

As Heather painstakingly crept forwards she could just barely make something out ahead of her–a faint, warm glow advancing from the other end of the hallway. "Justine?" Heather called out. "Wilma? Is that you, girls?"

A voice, dry and cracked like the rustling of dead leaves underfoot, came from the figure before her, "Oh no, dear. Not Mandy."

Heather's candle guttered and died so that the only light remaining was that slowly approaching glow. Eventually it was close enough to reveal its bearer's wizened features, their wispy grey hair, their diminutive, bird-like frame.

"Valerie?" asked Heather and the old woman gave a horse laugh. "In the flesh!" Valerie responded, "Such that it is." She smoothed her dress with a bony hand, her fingers trailing from her narrow, flattened chest right down to the jutting of her hip.

Heather's heart rate began to steady and her breathing calmed. So she was not facing some supernatural force or deranged criminal but an elderly woman. One that, in fact, she knew. Still, she was a little confused. "I thought you were on a cruise."

"No, dear," Valerie responded and clucked her tongue. "An elderly woman like me? I'm far too old to go off gallivanting around like that. Too old for a lot of things, really..." her voice trailed off wistfully, but she soon regained her focus. "Besides, someone has to take care of things around here."

As Valerie spoke, Heather found her eyes irresistibly drawn down to the ragged hem of the old woman's dress. There was something off about the garment, something that nagged at the edges of Heather's consciousness, but she could not quite pin it down. With every slight movement Valerie made, the hem shifted, almost as though her skirts were floating about her feet.

"Take care of things?" Heather echoed back vaguely, still appraising the dress. The fabric had a strange sheen to it, and it clung to Valerie's body in a way that Heather thought was unbecoming, even indecent, on an elderly lady. "What... what things?"

"Oh, the usual. Clean the house, prepare the meals. Taking care of him is a full-time job, you know."

Heather's eyebrows shot up in surprise, "Oh! I didn't realise that your husband. I mean. How is Jack?"

"Dear Jack's been gone for some six months now. I was referring to my other husband," explained Valerie.

"Other husband?" Heather's head swam dizzily and there came again that *scrape, scrape, scrape* from above.

"That's why you're all here tonight. Didn't you think it was odd that I let those two granddaughters of mine have run of my house?

"I'm getting old, you see. As soon as Jack passed on, I knew I wouldn't be far behind. It's time I got my affairs... *his* affairs... in order. The king needs someone to take care of him, you know. A new bride. Someone to keep him safe and well-fed. And to take care of the children, of course." at this, Valerie extended her free hand out towards Heather.

Heather leaned in to view Valerie's proffered palm and gasped when she saw several spiders wandering about on in. Valerie laughed her dry laugh and gently moved her hand against the wall, allowing the spiders to scuttle off. Heather saw in this an echo of Justine's earlier gesture and she felt a sudden rush of panic.

"Where are the girls?" asked Heather.

"The girls are fine," crooned Valerie. "They're all asleep. I saw to that. He only needs one bride, after all."

Listening to Valerie's high, strangely lilting voice, Valerie found herself growing drowsy again, despite the hammering in her heart and head. She blinked her heavy eyelids and looked down again at Valerie's dress. She saw several spiders of differing sizes running back and forth along the surface of the dress, all trailing long strands of silk as they went. They were spinning the dress, Heather realised. The whole thing was woven of cobwebs.

Valerie continued, “I had rather hoped he'd choose one of my granddaughters. It would be so much simpler if we could keep things in the family. But it's not them he's interested in.”

Heather's stomach dropped and she felt, in the empty pit of it, a surge of anger, “I won't let you touch Justine!”

“Oh no, dear,” Valerie replied, “Not Justine. He's chosen his bride.” With that she reached up with a withered hand and gently brushed aside the veil Heather had forgotten she was still wearing. Heather went to pull away the veil but found she could not move her arms. Panicked, she looked down and saw her wrists had been bound together by a mass of silk threads. Had all this happened while she had been listening to Valerie?

“No!” Heather cried and staggered backwards.

Valerie's voice grew suddenly harsh, “Now, don't be stupid! You should be honoured. You're going to be a queen, now.”

“But, Justine...the girls...”

"...will be fine as long as you come with me. Come. You don't want to leave your groom waiting any longer."

Heather thought of her daughter, lying somewhere asleep in that terrible house. She thought of Justine's upcoming wedding and of all the plans she had made with her new husband–their whole lives laid out ahead of them.

"If I come with you, they'll be safe?"

Valerie grinned, her face like a skull, "Of course!" she replied. "Really, you needn't make such a fuss. It's not as though you won't see her again. You're not losing your family. You're just gaining a new one."

Heather swallowed then nodded her head.

"There you go," said Valerie. "Now come with me up to the attic. He's waiting."

Valerie turned and headed back down the hallway and, after just a moment's hesitation, Heather followed. As they reached the stairs, Valerie began to sing softly–her voice strained and hoarse:

"The King has many names,
but I only call him 'love'
The King has many limbs, but
I need only cleave to one
The King has many eyes and
when he turns them all on me
I see reflected, many times, the
queen I'm meant to be."

Somewhere behind Valerie's strange singing, Heather heard the scraping grow gradually louder as they climbed the stairs towards the attic.

At the top of the stairs Valerie spun around and, reaching into Heather's pocket, pulled out the wrought-iron key. She unlocked the attic door and stepped aside.

The scraping had stopped now, to be replaced by a frenzied scurrying. Heather hesitated at the head of the stairs, but Valerie urged her onwards, waving at her with her free hand.

Heather felt strangely calm as she approached the room. She was not really sure what awaited her on the other side of that door or what her new life would be like. Looking down at her wrists Heather smiled grimly at the realisation that there was, as least, one thing she could feel certain of:

She was to wear silk to the wedding.

SISTER SCAVENGER

"THERE IS not!" Erin declared, catching the rubber ball and hugging it to her chest.

"There is, too!" insisted Kylie, raising her hands up in anticipation of Erin's next throw. "My sister told me. She's seen her."

Erin paused and considered this information carefully. Kylie's older sister, Sarah was usually a reliable source. She was in Year 8 after all, a big girl who went to the high school across the road. Erin chewed thoughtfully at her lower lip, so focused on this new revelation that she fumbled her next catch and had to stoop to pick the ball up from the wet grass.

Kylie continued, "Sarah says there's a real witch living there. She's a hundred years old, *two hundred*, and she has a pet crow and a black cat and... she eats children!"

This was going a little too far for Erin. She craned her neck to peer over the chain-link fence that separated the school's sports oval from the neat little house next door. It looked ordinary enough. The lace curtains in the two back windows were drawn closed and the garden plain, but well-kept.

"If the witch eats children," Erin reasoned, "Then how did Sarah get away?"

Kylie rolled her eyes at this self-evident question. "Because!" she spoke slowly, as if Erin were an idiot. "She did the sign of the cross before she went inside!" Erin had no rebuttal to this. "And she had her rosary beads in her pocket." Kylie added as an afterthought. "But mostly it was the sign of the cross."

The two girls tossed the ball back and forth in silence for a few moments– Erin as pensive as Kylie was smug.

Finally, Kylie spoke, "She's

probably watching us right now. And I'll bet she knows, too."

"Knows what?" Erin asked suspiciously.

"Knows that you're not a real catholic!"

Erin clutched the ball tightly and gritted her teeth. This was always a sore point with her. Although Erin's parents were both from Catholic families, and although they sent Erin to St Margaret's—the same school her mother had attended as a child—for some reason they had never had Erin baptised. She still attended church with her classmates and sang in the choir, but she always had this feeling of uneasiness, like she didn't quite belong.

In a fit of pique Erin threw the ball hard directly at her friend's face. Kylie squeaked and swatted at the ball with one hand, knocking it over the fence and into the garden next door. The two girls watched, mortified, as the ball bounced up the concrete path to the house and bumped against the back door.

The door creaked open, just a crack, and from the opening the girls could see one limpid eye blinking myopically at them. A claw-like hand–

as rough and mottled as a dead branch–emerged, grasped at the edge of the door, and slowly opened it with a high-pitched CR-REEEEEEEAK.

Erin and Kylie turned and bolted for the schoolhouse, their squeals and hysterical laughter piercing the dull April afternoon.

*

At dinner that night, in between heaping mouthfuls of shepherd's pie, Erin announced to her parents that, "I saw the witch that lives next to the school!"

"That's nice, kiddo," her father said, not looking up from his plate. Her mother frowned. "What witch?"

Her father quipped, "Shouldn't that be 'Which witch?'?"

Erin giggled. Her mother rolled her eyes but otherwise ignored him. She turned to face Erin directly, "What are you talking about, honey?"

Now it was Erin's turn to roll her eyes, "The witch! Everyone knows about her. She lives in the little house next to the school. The one with the lace curtains and the green back door."

Erin's mother's expression

remained blank for a few moments more before a grin spread across her face, "Are you talking about the convent?"

Erin shrugged. This wasn't a word she knew.

Her father let out a bark of a laugh, "A witch, eh? That sounds about right!" Her mother shot him a reproachful look, but she could not stop the corners of her mouth from twitching merrily.

"She's not a witch, Erin. She's a nun. Sister Matilda. She used to teach at St Margaret's back when I went to school there, before she got too old to teach anymore," Erin's mother grew suddenly thoughtful, her eyes glazing over as she toyed vacantly with one earring "Come to think of it, she was pretty old back then, too. She must be over ninety now!" She frowned again at this revelation, as though she felt the slow passage of years rushing up on her all at once.

Erin's father cut in, "Wait... *Sister Matilda*? Isn't she the one you used to call, *Sister Scavenger*?"

At this, Erin's mother's face immediately brightened, "That's right! She was always confiscating things: jewellery, toys, 'inappropriate' books. She would lock them all up in her desk drawer and then take them back to the convent with her after school... I never did get my jacks back. It didn't help that she looked like a vulture, too–all bent over and with that thin, crooked neck."

"Weren't some of your other teacher's nuns, too?" asked Erin's father as he served himself another helping of pie.

"Goodness, yes! Almost all of them, actually. And they all lived together in that little convent. Sister Matilda's the only one left, now."

Erin chased a pea around her plate with a fork as she contemplated her mother's words, "Sooo, she's not a witch?"

Erin's mother looked at her warmly, "No, honey. She's just a lonely old lady. You must leave her alone, though," she added sternly, "She's very old and she doesn't like to be bothered by children."

"Why did she become a teacher, then?" Erin asked, and her mother raised her eyebrows.

"Why did she become a nun, for that matter?" Erin's father added, but her mother could only shake her head and shrug. "Just promise me you won't bother her?" she asked Erin.

"I won't," Erin replied.

*

In morning classes the next day Erin watched, perplexed, as Kylie jiggled about in her seat. It seemed like her friend just couldn't keep still. She would keep turning to Erin as though about to say something but then, evidently thinking better of it, would just smirk annoyingly and go back to fidgeting. So distracted and disruptive was Kylie that morning that she almost got sent to the principal's office. The seriousness of this possible consequence was not lost on Kylie and she spent the rest of the class sitting on her hands in a marginally effective attempt to contain herself.

The bell rang for recess and Kylie sprang out of her seat and ran immediately over to Erin, dancing around impatiently as Erin packed up her pencil case and put her books under her desk. Out in the hallway Kylie grasped Erin's hand and, skipping, dragged her to where their backpacks were kept.

"Come on!" she urged Erin. "You have to see this!"

When they reached the backpacks,

lined up on a shelf beside all the others, Kylie became suddenly furtive. She held her backpack close to her chest and eyed the other children narrowly as they came up to collect their morning tea from their own bags.

Finally satisfied that they were not being observed, Kylie, with much ceremony, slowly opened the zipper on her backpack and reached into its polyester depths, withdrawing a book.

The book was small, but thick, with a glossy black cover stamped in foil. It was a library book, Erin knew from the Dewey decimal code pasted on its spine, but not from the school library. That much was obvious from the title: 'Halloway's Guide to Witchcraft and the Occult'.

Erin's heart skipped, and she looked about frantically for a few moments before snatching the book from her friend's hands. She scanned the title, and the pentagram emblazoned beneath it, several times before leaning in close to her friend and hissing, not without admiration, "How did you get that?"

Kylie smiled smugly, "My mum took be to the library yesterday. I just hid it between two chapter books and she didn't even notice." With that, Kylie reached into her bag again and withdrew two other books–a slim volume called 'Selby Speaks' and a slightly more ambitious work titled, 'Jet Smoke and Dragon Fire'. She took the book from Erin and sandwiched it between these other two.

"Mum said the house next door is a convent," Erin said as she and her friend wandered into the playground, "And that the old woman who lives there is a nun."

"A nun?" Kylie scoffed, "She didn't look like a nun! Where was her habit?"

She had a point, Erin realised. In movies nuns always wore black and white and a long veil, but the woman they had glimpsed reaching out from the back of the house wore no such thing. How could her mother have missed such an obvious point? Erin followed Kylie in moody silence as she considered this oversight.

After spending some time deciding on a suitably discreet spot, the pair settled on the dusty patch behind the bike-shed. Some older girls had taken up residence inside the shed, but they did not so much as look up as Erin and Kylie slipped around the corner and behind the tin edifice, there to crouch down in the dirt as they poured over Kylie's library book.

The book was quite detailed and, honestly, a bit beyond both of their reading levels, but they did manage to glean a few interesting bits of information. There was, for example, a whole chapter dedicated to 'the evil eye', which was a kind of curse a witch could cast just by looking at you, and Erin and Kylie spent some time carefully memorising some of the various ways to avert this curse (Kylie was particularly delighted with the advice that one should spit to avoid a witch's evil influence).

There were plenty of pictures, too. Many of the pictures featured old crones with crooked noses–sometimes standing above giant cauldrons, about to toss a baby inside, sometimes flying on broomsticks, sometimes cavorting with goats, or things very like goats. In a few of the pictures the women weren't wearing any clothes and Kylie giggled into her cupped palm whereas Erin just turned bright red and hurriedly skipped the pages.

Despite their limited understanding of the book, by the

time recess was over Erin and Kylie considered themselves experts on the topic of magic and the occult, and certainly up to the task of protecting themselves from any witch or other evil entity that they may encounter. Despite the reassurance from her mother that the woman next door was not a witch at all, Erin could not help but share Kylie's relief at having these new (well, old) charms and tricks at their disposal. Just in case.

*

Reading off a clipboard, Mrs Grafton announced brightly to the class that afternoon that it was Erin's turn to be school monitor.

Erin flushed. Most of her classmates were eager to take on the role of school monitor. Delivering messages and stationary supplies between the school's administration office and the staff lounge and the various classrooms not only meant getting out of class, it was also an invaluable opportunity to take a sticky-beak into what happens behind-the-scenes in the school. Where did the teachers go between classes? What were the strange markings on the blackboard in the year 6 class? Why did Mr Maloney need so many paperclips? These were questions to which only the school monitor held the key. Erin, however, did not relish the prospect of disturbing classes to deliver messages and supplies. She dreaded the abrupt silence when she knocked on the door, the impatience of the interrupted teacher, the dozens of eyes turned to watch her. Still, it was a role that was only offered to the most well-behaved and reliable students (Kylie, for instance, had never been monitor) and Erin could not really refuse. Dutifully, she trotted up to the front of the class and allowed Mrs Grafton to pin a little plastic name tag that read ‘MONITOR’ to her jumper.

Reporting promptly to the birdish Miss Flannigan, who presided over the school’s administrative affairs with a proprietary air, Erin received a stack of mail that needed to be delivered to the staff room, a box of fresh notebooks for class 4B, and a stern directive to “Hurry back.”

Erin made numerous other trips before she finally seemed to be through with her duties. With a sense of relief, Erin returned to the office with a hastily written thank you note for Miss Flannigan from Mr Morris then stood by meekly, waiting to be dismissed, while Miss Flannigan squinted at Mr Morris' scrawl.

Apparently satisfied, Miss Flannigan waved a hand at Erin and instructed her to, "Go back to class now."

Just as Erin turned to leave, Miss Flannigan called out hurriedly, "Wait! One last thing."

Her heart sinking, Erin turned back around and approached the desk. Miss Flannigan reached below it and brought up a package wrapped in brown paper. "This was delivered to the school by mistake. Could you be a dear and pop next door to give it to Sister Matilda?"

Miss Flannigan offered Erin one of her rare smiles, which is to say she pinched up the corners of her mouth and bared her teeth slightly. Erin shifted uncomfortably. Students weren't allowed off schoolgrounds during the day, so why was Miss Flannigan asking this of her?

She was asking this, Erin knew, for the same reason any adult ever asked something unfair of her: because they knew she would obey. Erin was angry at herself even as she accepted the package from Miss Flannigan and headed out the school's main entrance.

Erin was so wrapped up in her sense of injustice that she did not pay attention to her journey until she was standing on the doorstep of the convent next door. Erin hesitated. She did not want to meet Sister Matilda. Even if she wasn't the witch that Kylie claimed, her mother had warned her to keep away from the old woman. She gazed uneasily at the small house. Even in the middle of the afternoon it seemed dark and still. Perhaps Sister Matilda wasn't at home? This thought buoyed Erin, and without further hesitation she set the package down beside herself and smartly rapped on the door then, remembering what Kylie had said about Sarah, quickly performed the sign of the cross before picking up the parcel again.

A full minute passed and Erin, relieved, was just about to depart when she heard the clattering of multiple latches and dead-bolts and the front door slowly creaked open. "Yes, my child?" came a surprisingly steady voice from the doorway.

Kylie was right, Sister Matilda didn't look like a nun, but then she didn't look very much like a witch, either. Sure, she was old. Very old. The skin hung down from her curiously crooked neck in great folds and her eyes were dull and cloudy, but the malevolent impression was rather spoiled by a fluffy pink jumper and, around her neck, a pair of cats-eye glasses and a plain silver crucifix.

"This is for you," Erin announced shyly, lifting the parcel up high. Sister Matilda reached for her glasses and squinted through them at the offering. "Good, good," the nun murmured. "Bring it in for me, child." She shuffled into the house. Erin, trembling, followed.

The interior of the house was dimly lit and reminded Erin in some vague way of her grandmother's house. Except, where her grandmother collected antique dolls and souvenir spoons and displayed them all over her house, this place was crowded with holy pictures and religious figures.

There was one incongruous note among the harmony of icons, and it made Erin stop in her tracks. In the corner of the room was a gigantic cage.

It could easily house a person and Erin's mind immediately flew to the tale of Hansel and Gretel. "She's going to kill me!" Erin thought. "She's going to lock me in this cage and fatten me up to eat me!" Then, she heard a fluttering of feathered wings and saw a black beak and understood that this must be the cage where the witch kept her crow. But... wait... what was that glimpse of white? Erin moved in close to the cage and finally saw it's inhabitant, just as it began to let out a soft warble. Not a crow at all, then, but a magpie. Erin whispered, "Good afternoon, mister magpie." and felt immediate comfort.

"Put it on the table, there," Sister Matilda commanded with a dismissive wave. Looking around frantically, Erin saw a free spot on a low coffee table and placed the parcel there, next to a teapot in a knitted cosy.

With a heavy groan and an audible creaking of joints, Sister Matilda lowered herself into an armchair at the other side of the table to Erin. She picked up a still-steaming cup of tea and took a noisy sip. "Tea, child," she spoke. Erin did not drink tea (her parents said she was too young) but, again, this seemed more like an order than an offer. Erin saw a clean cup and saucer (at least, she hoped they were clean) beside the teapot and shakily poured herself half a cup then seated herself on a low, hard bench opposite Sister Matilda. Erin sipped at her tea politely and tried not to make a face as she swallowed the bitter liquid.

The two sat without speaking for several protracted minutes, the only sound that of Sister Matilda slurping at her tea and a faint clinking as the magpie shuffled up and down its perch.

"Did Agnes send you?" Sister Matilda asked casually.

"Ummm..." Erin stalled while her mind whirled busily. Who was Agnes?

"Agnes Flannigan," Sister Matilda added, as though she had heard what Erin was thinking. "She was always a good girl. Very pious. Very respectful. A good catholic girl."

"Oh, yes! Miss Flannigan sent me," Erin confirmed. Her heart raced guiltily at the reference to Miss Flannigan's religious inclinations and so, to cover her discomfort she added, "I'm school monitor today."

Sister Matilda grunted and nodded her head slowly. Silence settled again between the pair.

Eventually, Sister Matilda spoke again, "I knew your mother, you know."

Erin started, splashing a small drop of tea onto her saucer. "Don't look so surprised!" Sister Matilda scolded. "I knew everyone's mother! They all came here." Then, not quite under her breath, "Wilful, spoiled girls–the lot of them! Apart from Agnes, of course. Do you know what they called me?"

"No," Erin lied.

"'Sister Scavenger'. Tsk! And do you know why?"

Again, Erin shook her head.

Sister Matilda lay her teacup down and leant over the table towards Erin. "Would you like to see?" she hissed.

"She's going to kill me," Erin thought, again. Yet, still, she followed as the old woman led her down a dim corridor that smelled of incense. Obviously uneasy of her way, even in her own home, Sister Matilda leant her left hand against the wall to guide herself. It was not a long corridor, but every few steps Sister Matilda stopped to pat at the wall, mumbling to herself.

Finally they reached a plain white door with a brass knob and bolt-lock. Sister Matilda threw the lock then stepped back, motioning for Erin to go ahead of her. Erin hesitated. What could the old woman keep in that room? Her head spun with a dozen possibilities, all of them sinister. When she realised that she would not be free of Sister Matilda's milky gaze until she did something, however, she stepped forward and, trembling slightly, opened the door.

The room was small, but someone had made efficient use of the space. All the walls were lined from floor to ceiling with shelves. If there had once been a window, that too had been covered up with shelves. In the centre of the room were three free-standing shelves–the industrial kind you saw in a hardware store.

Erin's jaw dropped. Fear replaced with a quiet awe, she stepped into the room, unsure where to look first. The shelves were stacked full with a colourful array of objects. The treasures were so diverse and so eye-catching that they competed for Erin's attention, so that for several long seconds she could not pick out one item or another–just a beautiful blur of 'stuff'. It was like being in a museum. No, better than a museum. It was like being in the world's greatest toy store.

Eventually, as she made her way

into the room, Erin was able to make out specific objects–here was a bag of cats-eye marbles; there a doll in a blue dress. There were yo-yos and jacks; skipping ropes and slingshots.

"Do you like my collection?" Sister Matilda asked archly. "I've spent a lifetime amassing it. A rather long lifetime, at that. Girls were always trying to sneak things into school that they weren't allowed, but I had sharp eyes back then and nothing got past me."

Erin continued to wander through the room, her delight gradually giving way to a vague uneasiness. There was something off about the collection. True, the room was full of toys, costume jewellery and accessories, but scattered among the familiar object were a few that did not quite seem to fit–jars full of cloudy, viscous-looking fluids, bundles of hair, leather-bound books stamped with strange symbols.

Erin wanted to go back to school. As she turned to leave, she saw, out of the corner of her eye, another jar of marbles–this one full of the large ones she and her friends called 'bonkers'. Something made her stop, however, and inspect the jar more closely.

Erin froze. For one hysterical moment she thought of the cocktail onions her mother kept in a jar of vinegar in the fridge, but then her mind finally managed to process what she was looking at. The jar was full of eyes.

"None of them were right, you see," came Sister Matilda's voice from the doorway. "When my sisters died, I found some parts I could use–a kidney here, a liver there. By keeping all the best bits, I was able to outlive them all." She laughed a rich, almost musical laugh. "The eyes were no good, though," she continued. "They were all so old when they passed, and their vision was already fading. I need fresh, young eyes."

Erin tore her gaze away from the jar and looked up at Sister Matilda just in time to see her smoothly and quietly swing the door shut. Before Erin was even able to move Sister Matilda threw the bolt closed and then... and then there was no point in moving, really.

Of course, she tried. She threw her body against the door and beat at it with her tiny fists.

Once she had exhausted herself, Erin sank into a pile on the floor. "She's not going to kill me," she thought.

That's not what scavengers do, after all. She would leave her here, though, and in a few days, or perhaps even weeks, she would return to pick at what was left.

TROLL QUEEN

SHE WASN'T AS BAD as everyone says, not really.

Sure, she did kill that one guy—smashed him against the wall—but that was an accident. That was right at the beginning—when she first changed—and she didn't know her own strength yet. And, yeah, she did keep us locked in the office building for days, but that was to keep us safe. That's what she thought anyway.

I knew her, you know. Before she changed, I mean. Everyone knew her a little, of course. It's not a very big office.

I think, though, that I knew her best. But you don't want to hear about that. No one is interested in who she was. It's what she became that's got everyone worked up.

When she first began to change it happened very suddenly. She was sitting at her desk and went to stand up and just sort of... kept going?

No. That's not quite right. It was more like... like an accordion being extended. As she stood up, she just started to sort of unfold out of herself. She was a short woman, but within a few moments she was so tall that her head brushed the ceiling and she had to slouch down. Her hands were huge, as big as the computer monitors.

If you think about it, it must have been terrifying for her–which is probably why she struck out at Mark. She swung out at him when he started to scream. He was flung across the room so quickly and with such force that when he hit the wall he made a sort of wet thud. God. I can still hear it. His screaming stopped instantly.

Even in the fraction of a moment it had taken for Mark to be thrown across the room, she continued to change. Her limbs had all stretched and her hands and feet ended in sharp, curved claws. Her face had begun to elongate into a kind of muzzle. Most of her hair had come out and what was left hung from her head all lank and thin.

A tail started to sprout from the end of her spine. It hung limply behind her. She was starting to look like one of those ugly hairless cats, but grown monstrously large.

At the same time this was happening, the smog outside was turning that toxic purple colour and, at the other end of the office, people were starting to get reports coming in about what was going on. The office Wi-Fi was down, but people still had access to the internet on their phones.

The next few moments were sheer chaos. A message came over the loudspeaker, but I barely heard it. I was too focused on the transformation that was taking place right in front of me. It must have been something about an emergency lock-down because that's what happened next. All the electronic doors locked and the emergency warden came over from the other side of the office shouting that we had to "Shelter in place!" When he saw her, he froze on the spot and his shouts trailed off into a gurgle.

Everyone had stopped screaming. Someone—I think it was Inta—ran to the other end of the office to tell everyone what had happened. Some people were cowering under their desks, but the rest of us just stood there and stared. The sight of her standing there, on all fours, had us all transfixed. Her new form was horrible, but strangely compelling. I mean, she was just so big! She moved her neck–which was almost serpentine now–in a large arc and took in the room with eyes that swivelled about in their sockets. Finally, she spoke, in a voice completely unlike her old one. “Is everyone okay?” she asked.

Because that’s the thing, you see. Throughout the whole thing she really was concerned about our welfare. I don’t care what anyone else says. All she wanted to do was keep us safe.

*

In some places, I know, electronic doors are set to open if there is an emergency or the locks are physically damaged. Not in our office. We deal with 'Protected' information—really sensitive stuff—so if there was a problem with the locks then the doors would shut and have to be opened by one of the executive staff using their ID card and a thumb print. One of the first things she did was go around the whole office and destroy all the readers on the doors. Even if the lock-down was cancelled, there was no way we could get out without someone opening the doors from the other side. She tried to explain to everyone that we needed to keep away from the smog, but they were all too scared of her to listen.

It was the smog that had changed her. It was almost funny. She was usually one of the first people to arrive at the office in the morning but that day, for the only time ever, she was in late. She must have copped a real lungful of that stuff, because I remember her coughing and spluttering when she got in. We got only limited information coming in from outside about the smog. I remember words like, "unknown pathogen" and "genetic predisposition" and "mutagenic" being whispered about the office. I guess she was just one of the unlucky ones.

I'll admit, she did go kind of strange there for a bit. After a couple of days she seemed to get this idea that our muscles would become atrophied if we didn't exercise, so she cleared a space on the floor—pushing desks, chairs and computers aside into a pile—and made everyone stand there in a group and do exercises: callisthenics and such.

She got very excited when she found an old basketball that someone had kept at their desk. She called me over and told me I had to arrange for everyone to play a game. I started to tell her that I really only knew how to play rugby, not basketball, but this seemed to make her angry. She was literally quivering with rage and I could hear her teeth grinding together. After that I was pretty quick to agree to organise the game... and to do anything else she asked.

I heard a couple of people refer to her as, “The troll”. I didn’t like that. She couldn’t help what she’d become. She couldn’t help that we were afraid. It wasn’t just fear that made us do what she wanted, though. By the end of it we wanted to. The blokes did, at least.

You see, whenever people were getting too restless or scared or angry, she would release this gas. We seemed to be safe from the smog outside, but the office soon became suffused with this other gas. It came out of these vents that ran all the way down her... I guess you'd call them, “flanks”? The vents looked almost like open wounds: pink and wet and gaping. They would purse and pucker and you would see the gas seeping out like smoke.

The smell? It’s hard to describe. I guess you’d say it was sort of salty—like the beach—but there was this undercurrent of sweetness. The women liked the smell. Janine said it made her feel languid and sleepy and, judging by their behaviour, the rest of them must have felt the same. The other men, though!

A few just got all placid like the women, but the rest went crazy whenever that gas started to pump out of her. Maybe it was like that stuff insects use: 'pheromones', is it? Certainly, whatever it was made most of the other guys get all hot and bothered, if you know what I mean.

And (how can I put this delicately?) despite the fact that she had grown so huge, some parts of her had sort of... remained the same size. That place between her legs (her hind legs, yes) was still as small and as sweet as any man could ask for and, boy, did they just line up to use it. She would squat down and the guys would all take turns entering her from behind.

I say, 'take turns'. Sometimes, when too many were under the effect of that gas, they'd get impatient and some would just use the vents along her side instead. She didn't seem to mind.

Oh, of course I had a go, too. That was different, though. The smoke didn't effect me. I loved her. And why not? Didn't you see her? She was magnificent! And, besides, she loved me more than the other guys. I could tell.

And then you lot came and broke down the doors and that's how you found us–the women: peaceful; the men: spent. You must have got a shock when you saw her. She didn't waste a second, though. As soon as you started pouring through that door she turned and burst through one of the windows as if that tempered glass was no tougher than toffee. She fell the seven stories to the ground and landed on all-fours like a cat.

I saw her loping off into the smog like a wounded animal. No, I don't know where she headed, and I wouldn't tell you if I did. People say she was a monster. If that's true—and I'm not sure that it is—she must have been the queen of all monsters.

THE OTHER GRACE

I'VE ALWAYS HAD AN uneasy relationship with mirrors, although I suppose that's not unusual for a girl. I remember when I was little and had to get out of bed during the night for a glass of water or to use the toilet, I would always race past the large mirror in our bathroom with eyes screwed tightly shut. I never knew exactly what it was that frightened me so. Was I afraid I'd see the reflection of something lurking behind me? Did I see mirrors as some otherworldly portal to another realm? I'm just not sure. All I know is that I found something ominous about a mirror's smooth, cold surface–particularly by night.

When I was seventeen my parents renovated our house. Dad agreed to the renovation only under duress, eventually giving in to Mum's complaints about how the place was so old it was falling apart; that things kept breaking and she could hear strange noises at night that must have been caused by subsidence.

As part of the whole process they installed built-in wardrobes in all the bedrooms. What they hadn't told me is that the sliding doors of the wardrobes would be mirrored–meaning one entire wall of my bedroom was to be covered in a reflective surface from floor to ceiling. How could I tell them that I still held some of that childish dread of mirrors by night?

Worse still, now that I was a teenager, I'd discovered the other sinister aspect of mirrors. In the days after they installed the built-in wardrobe in my room, I would spend ages staring critically at my own reflection–cursing every roll of fat about my middle and each freckle on my piebald face.

Around that time, we had one of

those self-esteem coaches come and talk at our school. She insisted that one of the best approaches to body acceptance was to 'Become friends with your reflection'... that is how she put it. While seeming to stare directly at me she spoke about affirmations and positive self-talk. She even recommended spending five minutes a day standing naked in front of a mirror until what we saw was no longer alien to ourselves. My classmates had snickered at this suggestion and I joined them, but that afternoon when I got home, I stripped down to my underwear and stood in front of my bedroom mirror.

Thinking carefully about what the coach had said about the kind of language to use when addressing ourselves, I declared, "You are a worthy manifestation of the divine", then giggled uneasily before muttering, "You are an ugly dork."

I took a deep breath, tied back my hair and tried again. *It's not so bad, is it, this form I'm confronted with?* I thought to myself. *The freckled features; the doughy figure. Surely I can learn to live comfortably in this skin?*

Sighing again, I stepped toward the mirror, pressed my hands against the silvered glass, leant in close and shut my eyes. After a moment's hesitation my puckered lips found the cold surface of the mirror and lingered there in a frozen kiss.

For some time I remained in this position, eyes closed tight, until my head grew strangely dizzy and I felt as if I was sinking into the mirror, as if it's surface was shifting and rippling about me like water. Then, I felt something clutch at my wrist and my eyes flew open in surprise...

*

...I was lying on my back in bed. Disoriented, wondering if my experience with the mirror had been a dream, I rolled over. My alarm clock showed that it was 7.30am. I sat bolt upright. How could that be? It had been no later than 4.30 in the afternoon when I had undressed in front of the mirror. What had happened after that?

Trying to calm down, I took slow, steady breaths and attempted to reconstruct the previous day in my head. I remembered getting up and dressed, having breakfast, going to school, the special assembly with the motivational speaker, getting home and standing in front of the mirror and then... nothing! Where had the evening gone?

Shakily, I got out of bed and dressed myself for school, trying to reassure myself that my memory would come back as soon as I was properly awake. As I reached for my glasses, I found an envelope sitting in the middle of my bedside table. I picked up the envelope and turned it over, squinting at the scrawl on its cover. After putting on my glasses I was (just barely) able to make out my own name scribbled in a shaky, but oddly familiar, hand. Opening the envelope, I found a single piece of paper on which was written in the same, barely legible script, the words:

You're welcome.

Puzzled, but anxious not to miss the school bus, I stuffed the cryptic note into my backpack and rushed out the door, shouting a quick, "See you later!" as I passed my mother in the kitchen. She looked like she was about to say something, but I hurried on, pretending not to notice.

I arrived at school with no clearer

recollection of the night before and things were still a blank well into third period. All the while that Mrs Metcalf lectured, I chewed on the edge of my pen and fretted about the lapse in my memory. Was I suffering some rare kind of adolescent dementia? Had I had one of those fugue states?

So fixated was I on these musings that I didn't even notice Mrs Metcalf was calling my name until she finally snapped shrilly, "Miss Jones! If you can tear your attention away from the window for one minute and join us here in the classroom!"

I dropped my pen and turned to stare at Mrs Metcalf slackly. "Huh?"

"Your homework, Grace," Mrs Metcalf continued pointedly, her right arm extended towards my desk. "Or are we to have another of your famous excuses?"

"Ummm..." I had completely forgotten about last night's homework... not that I had been planning on doing it anyway. As I struggled to search for an excuse Mrs Metcalf pointed down at my desk and asked, "Is that it?"

Surprised, I looked down at a sheet of paper that was sticking out of the pages of my English textbook.

"Y-yes?" I ventured, allowing Mrs Metcalf to withdraw the sheet of paper, then peer at it sceptically. "My!" she eventually declared. "Wonders will never cease!" She strode over to the next desk, leaving me baffled but relieved.

I drifted through the rest of the school day in a dull haze, not really listening to my teachers or engaging with my classmates. I was not sure what the document was that I had handed over to Mrs Metcalf or where it had come from. The only certainty I had was that it was not the essay on To Kill a Mockingbird that had been due that day. I had written no such thing, though I'd read the book. Enjoyed it, in fact. I had lots of thoughts about the characters and themes Harper Lee had woven into her narrative, but when it came to actually writing them down I just... couldn't. As with everything else those days I just lacked any motivation. Sometimes I felt like it was all I could do to drag myself out of bed in the morning.

I was not surprised, therefore, when Mrs Metcalf tracked me down after final period and lured me back to her office.

"This essay of yours..." Mrs Metcalf

began after I sat down opposite her desk. "Yes," I replied mechanically, gazing at a poster just behind Mrs Metcalf's shoulder and already beginning to tune out.

"...It's some of the best work I've seen from you in a long time."

My attention snapped back like a rubber band. "Sorry?"

"True, it's not exactly what the assignment called for–I did ask for a deconstruction of the character of Atticus Finch–but your exploration of the concept of fear in the novel was... surprisingly insightful. I can't say I entirely agreed with all your points, but you constructed a cogent and compelling argument, nonetheless. I just wanted to pull you aside to congratulate you on your good work. I hope to see more of the same from you in future." She handed back the essay, marked with a red 'A'. I frowned, remembering a time, only recently, when Mrs Metcalf had quipped during class that I, "Probably didn't even remember how to spell 'A'". None of this made any sense.

Mrs Metcalf looked suddenly stern, "Is there something you want to say Grace?"

"N-no." I stammered, "I just... Thank you."

The teacher beamed, "You're welcome. Now off you go. I have more essays to mark."

On the bus ride home, I could barely tear my attention away from the essay. I must have read and re-read it a dozen times. I didn't remember writing the essay but, by the time I arrived home I felt sure of one thing–I had written it. The ideas were all things I had thought of when reading the book and it was all expressed in a language and style that was unquestionably my own. It may have been months since I had taken the effort to produce any work, but I still recognised my own style. The handwriting, though messy, was also recognisably mine.

There was something else, too. Mrs Metcalf was right–the essay really was insightful. Seeing my thoughts carefully laid out on paper before me I could appreciate the depth and potential of my own ideas.

The only answer I could come up with was that I must have written the essay last night at some point during the time I had forgotten. There was something else that was bothering me, though. Something that Mrs Metcalf had said was gnawing at the edges of my consciousness. What was it?

You're welcome.

I threw my backpack off and began rummaging through it until I found the note I had shoved in there that morning. It had become creased and a little piece of it had torn off the corner, but I brought it over to my desk and flattened it out as best I could. 'You're welcome', that simple message scrawled in blue pen–a messy imitation of my own writing, I saw now–was the only thing written on the paper.

I could feel the little hairs at the back of my neck stand on end and I had the eerie sense that someone was watching me. I looked behind my back, but the door to my bedroom was closed. I turned back around swiftly and looked in the mirror but all I saw, of course, was my own reflection. I frowned, and it seemed there was a delay–just a fraction of a second–before my reflection frowned back at me. I closed my eyes and rubbed them furiously...

*

...It was morning. I sat bolt upright

in bed. "No!" I gasped, clutching at my chest. I tossed my blankets aside and sprung out of bed, looking about myself frantically. My eyes finally rested on my bedside table, where there lay another note.

I picked it up. The writing, though still a little shaky, looked noticeably neater than in the previous note and looked more identifiably my own:

> *Good morning my dearest Grace,*
> *Thank you so much for the wonderful evening.*
> *I look forward to doing it all again tonight.*
> *Faithfully yours,*
> *The other Grace*

I stared at the note slack jawed. I looked up and my eyes caught my own reflection in the mirror. I frowned, but this time my reflection did not frown back. I watched, stunned, as the figure in the mirror raised one eyebrow archly. Frozen to the spot, I raised one hand to my face. My reflection grinned.

It was even harder than usual to focus at school that day. I was plagued by the one, persistent thought - "Am I going crazy?"

When I went through my backpack I found that, once again, my English homework had been completed. It was a creative writing project. Mrs Metcalf had tasked us all with writing a description of someone we knew in the style of any literary genre we chose. Heart thudding, I took the piece of paper into the girls' toilets where I could read it in private:

Grace Jones
Year 11 English
Genre Writing Project– Romance

Her eyes are grey and, though she thinks them dull, I see in those pale irises a world of depth and feeling. A mass of storm clouds, ever shifting and changing, brimming with the promise of sweet showers or heavy, drenching rain. I long to be soaked through.

When her eyes meet mine, they glitter with humour. I fancy I see a flash of silver radiate from the core. My pulse quickens.

She moves with a kind of awkward charm and I try my best to mimic her. Like a pair of courting sea-dragons–fragile; lonely–we are locked in this strange dance.

We kiss. Her lips are trembling as they meet my own. I am as cold and hard as ice but she thaws me.

I wonder if she will ever see me as clearly as I see her and, at the same time, I know it does not matter as long as I can continue to see myself like this–reflected back in the dark pools of her pupils...

I stopped reading, my face flushed pink. I couldn't hand this in! Mrs Metcalf would throw a fit.

I pictured the face of my conservative, catholic English-teacher as she read the piece of writing I held now in my hands. Despite myself, I began to smirk. It might be funny, after all, just to see how Mrs Metcalf would respond to the piece. The smirk became a grin and I emerged from my stall committed to follow through with this. As I passed the sinks, I caught my reflection in the mirror and noticed that my eyes did seem to glitter, after all.

The elation I felt at my tiny rebellion was short-lived, however, and by the time the final bell rang it was only reluctantly that I made my way to the bus stop. In truth I was nervous about what was waiting for me at home. I kept thinking about the mirror. I couldn't help but wonder whether there really was something lurking on the other side.

...The other Grace

Once home I entered my bedroom almost at a run, rushing past the mirror with my eyes downcast before reaching my bed and sitting down deliberately. I had decided what I was going to do.

Reaching into my backpack I pulled out a leaf of foolscap paper and, leaning against my maths textbook, began to write:

Who are you, really? Are you a ghost? A demon?

I chewed at the end of my pen, carefully considering my next line:

What do you want from me?

My missive (such as it was) complete, I grabbed a piece of sticky-tape, turned around and strode up to the mirror. I taped my sheet of paper to the mirror then glared at my reflection–silently challenging it.

I don't know how long I stood there. After a while I gave up on the impossible staring-contest and turned my attention to the rest of my reflected form. I tutted in distaste as I went through the familiar process of reviewing my body–the too soft belly, the too small breasts, the too freckled skin. I went to lean against the mirror with one hand, and that is when I noticed something. They were delicate, my hands. One might even say elegant. How had I never noticed that before?

Enthralled, I stared at my hand while slowly tracing patterns on the mirror. I blew a fog onto its surface with my breath then traced a love heart around my face. From the centre of the heart, my reflection blew a kiss at me.

I gasped, although honestly I was only a little surprised. That unsolicited action by my own reflection only confirmed what I had already suspected–there really was something there. I pressed both palms flat against the mirror and leant in close. "Show me." I urged. After a few moments I felt as though my hands were sinking into the mirror–like it had become a viscous fluid. Then there was the sensation of someone grabbing my arm. I closed my eyes, partly from fear, but mainly with a sense of calm resignation.

*

When I awoke the next morning, I was not concerned or even surprised. Rather, I felt... elated! I sat up in bed and immediately patted eagerly at my bedside table until I finally found what I was looking for–an envelope!

Darling Grace,

I wish I could answer your first question, but the truth is I don't remember who or what I was before I was you. I can't imagine even wanting to be anything else.

As for your second question, the truth is you have already given me so much. You have shared your home, your mind, your body. I have spent the last few nights getting to know you as best I could. If there was just one more thing I wanted from you, it would be to know you more.

Take me with you. Please.

Faithfully yours,
The other Grace

I fell back to the bed, clutching the letter to my breast as I stared at the ceiling. For the first time I became truly conscious of the fact that I was not a happy person. It wasn't just that I didn't like my body or that I was ostracised by my classmates and teachers alike. Deep down I felt fundamentally flawed, like I was a mistake the universe had made. But then, there were those words:

...I can't imagine even wanting to be anything else.

I sat up. Whoever or whatever this "other Grace" from the beyond the mirror was, I had to try and find a way to take them with me.

I rummaged around in the cupboard under the bathroom sink until I found what I was after–a small plastic compact containing some pressed powder blush and, more importantly, a small mirror. Leaving the cupboard in disarray, I rushed back to the bedroom with my prize.

Trembling with anticipation I stood once more in front of my bedroom mirror. I wasn't at all sure what I was doing, but everything about this situation so far had been so surreal that I figured it didn't hurt to try one more unlikely thing.

With this in mind, I opened up the compact and turned it to face the bedroom mirror. I twisted it this way and that, arranging it so that I could see a seemingly endless string of reflections echoing back at each other between the two mirrors. It was like a long, glass corridor stretching out into infinity, seeming to diminish as it went along, but never entirely vanishing. As I stared deeply into that vast hallway, I finally made out one tiny discrepancy in the otherwise perfectly repeating pattern–a tiny, dark form several dozen reflections back that seemed to be moving closer. I watched, transfixed, as the figure continued to advance towards me through the string of reflections. As it got gradually closer I began to feel dizzy, like I was falling into the reflection myself. I reached out and braced myself against the wardrobe door with my free hand. As the figure drew ever closer I felt a swelling in my chest and gasped for air.

*

Waking up the next morning I did not feel even slightly disoriented. "I'm beginning to get used to this," I thought. The feeling of fullness in my chest was still there and I smiled, thinking to myself, "They're here. With me." I was unsurprised to find the compact sitting on my bedside table with a note underneath it:

My Grace,

I am so looking forward to today!

Thank you so much.

Faithfully yours,
The other Grace

I smiled softly to myself then, getting dressed, slipped the compact into my pocket and headed off for school. Just as I was about to head out the front door my mother burst out from the kitchen looking anxious. "You won't be late from school this afternoon, will you?" she asked. "N-ooooo," I replied guardedly. As I spoke, I fingered the compact in my pocket.

She sighed. "Good! We're having a family meeting as soon as you get home. Don't forget!"

"Sure." I mumbled, "Bye, Mum!" then I rushed out the door.

I had expected to be distracted all day, but, if anything, I was better able to concentrate in class than I had been in months. Whenever I felt anxious or uneasy, whenever I felt snubbed by a teacher or excluded by my classmates, I just touched the compact in my pocket, or brought it out to rest inconspicuously among the clutter on my desk, and smiled to myself. Occasionally, when I was certain of not being noticed, I would flip open the compact and glance at the reflection. Sometimes, the face I saw there would bat its eyelashes at me, or smirk knowingly and I would have to cover my mouth to stifle a giggle.

On the bus trip home from school I thought about all the places I could take the other Grace over the weekend–the shopping centre, maybe, or the local library–all my usual haunts. I smiled at that, and was still smiling when I arrived home to find my parents sitting at the dining-room table with a man I didn't know.

Mum stood up as I entered, "You're here!" she cried. I could see bags under her eyes and noticed, for the first time, how drained she looked. Dad was staring silently at the table as he sat there, and the strange man was unpacking various items from a large briefcase.

"Come, Grace," Mum said, her tone hushed but oddly excited. She grabbed my hand and lead me to the table. "Sit here, next to me. This is Mr Gregson." The strange man nodded perfunctorily, still busy arranging the items he had unpacked on the table in front of him, "He's going to help us with... our little problem." Dad scoffed at this. Mum shot him an angry look and he went back to staring at the table.

Uneasy, I sat down as Mum continued, "You must have noticed, sweetie, that things... haven't been right around here for a little while now."

I thought about this carefully, but all that really came to mind was that, lately, Mum and Dad seemed to have been arguing a lot more than usual.

"Things going missing or moving about. The footsteps up and down the corridor at night. I know your father thinks I'm just imagining things or getting forgetful—" there was a grunt from Dad's end of the table, but no further comment, ".— but Mr Gregson here is an expert in these things and he says there's definitely a— a presence here." My hand went instinctively to grip at the compact in my pocket. "—And he's here to help us get rid of it."

Mr Gregson smiled amiably at me. "It's a simple procedure, really, and now that we have the whole family here, we can get started. Please, young lady, take a seat."

"I... I don't know about this." I said and began to back away from the table. "You're not the only one," grumbled Dad.

"Please, Grace." my mother implored, her voice sounding shaky and strained, "Just sit down."

What choice did I have? I took my usual seat at the table and we all joined hands as Mr Gregson led us through his strange ritual.

I remember little of what happened. There was a flickering candle, some muttered words read from an old book, the ringing of a silver bell then a tightness in my chest followed by a heart-breaking feeling of lightness. I felt empty.

Afterwards I ran to my room and slammed the door. I went right up to the mirror but all I saw there was my own anxious expression. Frantically I dug the compact out of my pocket, but my reflection in it seemed likewise flat–without depth or dimension.

For the first time in days I remembered every minute of my evening. I spent the whole night crying.

*

I still carry the compact with me. I will pull it out from time to time, ostensibly to fix my hair or check my makeup, but really I am looking for that tell-tale smirk of the lips or flutter of the lashes.

The truth is I miss them every day, that other Grace. As time goes by, though, I find it gradually easier to cope. It's as though I've discovered an inner strength that wasn't there before. I'm alone now... but that's okay. After all, they taught me how to love myself.

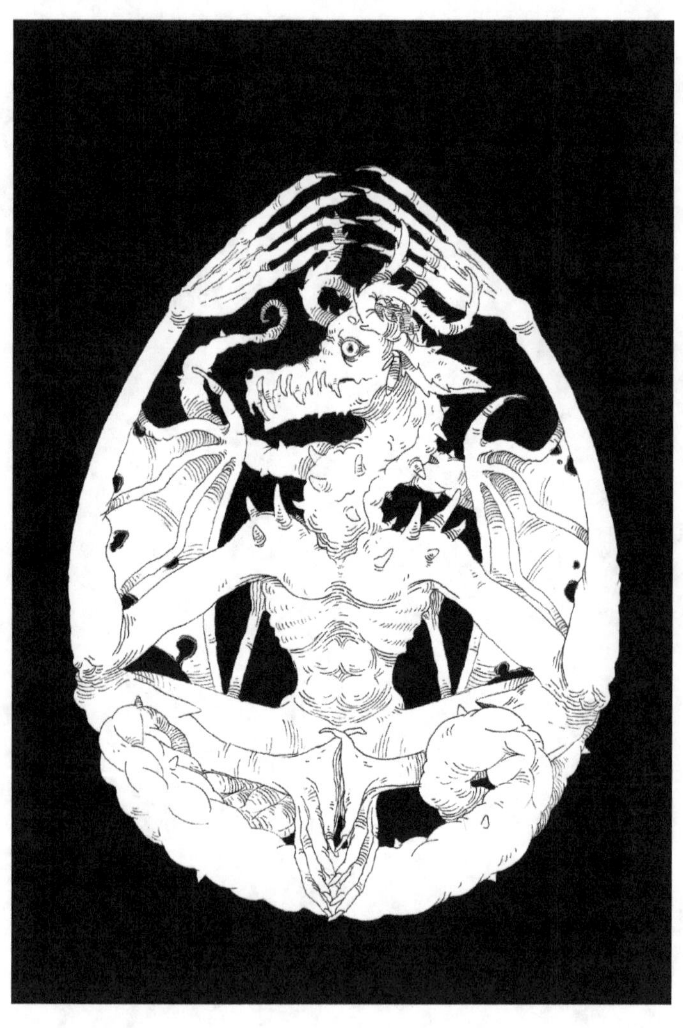

UNDER THE BED

SOMETHING STIRRED inside the wardrobe.

Lying stiff in her bed, the young girl watched as strange shadows slipped across the walls of her room. This twilight hour, eerie in the uncertain play of light and darkness, was always her most hated time of day, for she fancied that she saw in the surrounding shadows the forms of those demons who haunted her nights and forced her into restless, unnatural sleep. Nervous eyes darted about, finally resting on the door of the wardrobe, slightly ajar. The girl let out a scream, but the sound caught in her throat and came out as a gurgle, muted by the large down doona she had pulled up to cover half of her face.

When the door to her room opened, letting in a stream of white light, the girl was still lying transfixed. "Are you okay, Precious?" came the voice from the light–velvety and soothing.

The child relaxed slightly at the familiar sound, then turned to face the stream of light. "M-mummy! I'm scared!" she said, beginning to cry.

"Shhh, Precious, shhh," came the mother's soothing voice. "What are you afraid of?"

Swallowing her sobs, the child looked back toward the wardrobe. She whispered, "There are monsters in the cupboard."

The child's mother chuckled softly, moving toward the side of the girl's bed. "Oh, I don't think you have to worry about monsters in the wardrobe." She sat down and began smoothing the wrinkled pink tulips of the doona with her hand then, after a pause, leant in toward the little girl. "You don't ever have to worry about monsters in your wardrobe because, if any monsters do try to bother you, then the dragon under your bed will eat them up."

There was silence for a moment as the

child digested these words. The mother sat up again, straight-backed, and continued flattening out the doona. There was a note of fear in the girl's voice when next she spoke. "Dragon? Like the one in my picture book?"

The mother picked up the book that lay beside the child's bed and examined the pictures critically. She stopped at one; a gleaming white knight battling an emerald dragon. The creature was magnificent. Fire poured from its open jaws and its grand wings were spread in an attitude of flight. She returned the book to its place. "Oh, don't worry," she said matter-of-factly, patting the bed. "The dragon may be strong and powerful like the ones in your books, but it's a good dragon. Your very own dragon."

Leaning over the side of the bed, the girl lifted its ruffled skirt as though to peek but thought better of it. "Under my bed?" she queried.

Her mother nodded and left the room without another word, taking the stream of light with her as she closed the door.

Confused, but significantly less afraid, the girl wriggled back under her covers, closed her eyes and whispered tenderly into the night, "Protect me, dragon."

As she rolled over to settle into sleep the bedsprings whined and groaned, mingling with her gentle breathing to form a quiet melody.

And that was my first lullaby.

I live in an obsolete space, a space only defined by its relation to other objects. On top of the carpet. Under the bed. I do not remember a time before this life under the bed. As far as I know I have always been here. This was my nursery. This is my home.

There is very little room here for me and what little space I have is shared with broken toys and tattered books and a host of other half-forgotten items. To fit I must crouch down as much as possible. Forever hunched in this awkward pose, my limbs have become deformed. I am an ugly, wretched, twisted figure who should have been great.

It was, I think, the mother who called me here, unknowingly dragging me from the depths of oblivion. I was a joke, something created by the mother to soothe her frightened child. The mother made me up and the child believed her and so I was real. Such is the power of a child's faith. Sometimes when I would hear the mother talking about me in her bedtime stories to the child, when I heard the word '"dragon" falling from her lips, I would fear that I had been discovered. Then I would realise that she was just playing a game. That I was not real to her. Sometimes, that frightened me, too. Sometimes it just hurt.

I did not want them to find me, but keeping my form hidden was no easy task and so, as a matter of necessity, I developed an immense talent for folding myself. I can fold myself upward, inward, beneath my mangled wings. Folded once I take the appearance of a crumpled pile of clothes. Folded twice I am some discarded doll or teddy-bear. Again and again I fold myself until I fold up into the shadows themselves.

My purpose in life is simple. From my first moment of consciousness I knew by a feeling in my bones, a stirring in my blood, that I must protect the girl. I was to lay here, to watch and to wait, my lidless eyes fixed on the crack under the wardrobe door. They only come at night, those strange creatures that it is my duty to destroy. They slip through the slit beneath the wardrobe door–silent and sly.

Sometimes, with the larger ones especially, I would leap out at them from beneath the bed. Wrapping my body around them I crushed them until there was nothing left but a pile of dust and bones and their tortured wails, which soon disappeared into the air. More often, though, all I was ever required to do was lie patiently and lure them under the bed and into my waiting jaws.

On some quiet nights when the wardrobe was still, and the moon was high I would abandon my vigil and climb up the metal posts of the bed to gaze upon the girl as she slept. This is, in fact, one of my earliest memories.

I remember the first night I looked upon her. I had been waiting for hours that night and there was no hint of my enemies. There had never been a night like this, where there was not at least some small threat for me to vanquish. I grew restless and uneasy and at last made up my mind to visit my ward, that my eyes might see what it was I was fated to protect. Cautiously at first, I inched myself out from under the bed, hearing joints pop with every movement. The window had been left open that night, but the breeze was so faint that there was only the slightest disturbance in the lace curtains. Dew had gathered in the corners of the windowpane, glittered with the promise of frost. I began to wind myself up and around the dull brass of the girl's bedpost until I could view her.

I couldn't breathe, my chest tightening like the skin of a drum. There lay the girl, so close I could touch her, so close I could feel her breath on the tip of my nose. With the pallid light of the moon resting on her gentle face the girl looked like some ethereal creature, some angel carved of pearl. I leant in close and whispered dreams into her ears.

My fights with the wardrobe creatures continued, and I have become well-versed in the visceral secrets of their monstrous anatomy. I know the locations of all the vital organs and the tender regions of flesh through which they can be readily accessed. I know, too, those parts which inflict the most pain — that to pull an imp's tail will send it into a convulsive fit, whereas gremlins are especially delicate about the webbing between their nimble fingers.

I am a particular expert on devils — those long, lean creatures with pointed tails and forked tongues. I nearly lost my life to such a creature. It had slunk out of the wardrobe on all-fours, moving with the grace of shadows. It moved so silently that I had not known of its presence until I smelt the sulphur on its breath, and by then it was squatting right beside me. I remember turning and sinking my teeth into its arm, only to release it with a jerk. The devil's skin was slick with poison. "You should be more careful, brother," the devil hissed, then with a laugh bounded back into the open wardrobe. All night I lay there — defeated, barely conscious — my body still trembling from the poison and the devil's words still echoing in my ears. On later nights I was more wary of such devils, though their visits were rare. I would spend long hours studying their lithe and toxic bodies in meticulous detail.

During the day there is very little for me to do. I have no need for sleep, as such, but I spend most of the day dozing, out of boredom. Sometimes I roll onto my back and count the stitches in the mattress. Repeated on the mattress is a single, indecipherable pattern of pointed symbols. I have spent hours contemplating these symbols, waiting for some meaning to emerge from the weave. All I learnt is that three hundred and ninety-six stitches make up this mysterious pattern of:

Australian Osteopathic Association.

As for the mattress as a whole, well, to this day I do not know how many stitches make up its total because I am forever losing my count part way through and must start from the beginning.

Sometimes, when she was young, the girl would creep into the room on tiptoes, tittering softly under her breath, and come up right to the edge of the bed. In a clumsy flurry of movements, she would then lift the bed skirt and yell "For you!", throwing handfuls of golden-brown cereal under the bed. "Cornflakes" she called them. The cereal was crispy and would get stuck between my teeth, but I liked it. At nights she would murmur to me as she drifted off to sleep, just as she did that first night, asking me to protect her.

One day, urged on by what I had seen of the girl lying in her bed at night, and by her kindness to me, I grew bold and decided it was time to show myself to the girl.

When the girl left for school in the morning I began to prowl about her room until she returned. Emerging from under the bed, I stretched out my stiff limbs feeling the blood rush to my extremities. There were drawers to paw through, crammed with bright pieces of clothing, notebooks filled with more strange symbols and, hidden throughout, multicoloured blobs of something sweet-smelling and sticky. The room seemed so big and so empty and I felt exposed and anxious. I looked about for something to distract myself with. In the far corner of the room was a large, flat surface — a thin sliver of frozen water propped up against the wall. I began to move toward the object and realised that is was not made of ice, but glass. Another window?

Before me I saw a pile of scales, bones and sinewy muscles. The scales, a deep purple colour, seemed to be flaking off and beneath them the pinkish flesh was oozing with various fluids. The figure before me had wings, too, albeit so crippled that they had no visible use. Dun membrane was pulled so tight across the metacarpal bones that I could see the throbbing network of veins beneath. Snaking out from behind the creature was a twitching, fleshy tail; so long I could not see its tip.

Hideous! Malformed! The creature was all pointed and jagged, with claws, horns and needle-like teeth jutting out from the most unlikely places. It looked as vile as any monster I had sent to screaming death.

And the creature's head! Large ears, torn and crusted with blood, hung down from the side of its long, pointed face. Watery, almost colourless eyes returned my own gaze. The creature seemed sad.

I continued to stare at the figure before me until, gripped with a sudden fear I turned away and looked instead at the wardrobe door and shuddered. I knew that the figure behind the glass was my own reflection. My frenzied eye rolled about to take in the rest of the room. Its brightness and its beauty shamed me now, and I skulked back to my space between the mattress and the floor, feeling as though I had fouled some sacred place. I would never again venture out during the daylight; I would never let the little girl see me.

As the girl grew older, she gradually forgot to feed me stolen Cornflakes. I must content myself now with eating the wardrobe-monsters. After I have done with their stringy meat, I spend days sucking at their bones for the marrow. Truth be told, I don't require a lot of nourishment and often survive on the filmy layers of dust that gather on the bedposts and the dirt and crumbs that sink into the fibres of the carpet. But the taste is bland, and I miss the Cornflakes.

I remember the first night the girl forgot to ask for my protection. I was crouched beneath the mattress, waiting to hear her whisper. My whole body quivered in anticipation of that prized moment of contact between me and my ward, but she never spoke my name. All I could hear through the thick night air was her soft sigh as sleep took her, a chorus of crickets chirping outside and my own heart thundering in my ears: I knew it to be broken.

Then, I fear, she forgot me altogether. Sometimes in her sleep the girl would whimper in fear and loneliness. I don't think she knew why.

Now the girl rarely stays here. Her bed, still made, still neat, lies empty above me. No longer do the mattress springs sing to welcome her into their embrace; no longer does her own faint breathing resonate in my ears. These sounds are replaced by the crickets and the lace curtain shifting in the night breeze.

I am not always alone, though. The rhythms of the bedroom go on, ignorant of its mistress's absence. Small signs of life continue. Once a tiny spider, mistaking my inertia for lifelessness, spun her web from my brow bone to the tip of my snout, the threads tickling my nostrils. I like to watch the spiders as they spin their dainty webs. Peering closely at the patterns made of the fine strands of silk I can see the whole universe displayed — all its intricacies unfolded in these strange schemata. I wait till the very moment when the spiders have finished their elaborate creations, and then I eat them, for what is their point anymore?

Time wears on and my body seems to rot around me. Membrane pulls so tight it tears, bones hollow, blood ceases its flow altogether. I still wait here, though. I wait because it is my job, and I know that, one day, the girl will come back for me. And so, I lay here and I watch and I wait, the dust settling upon my ruined body like a shroud. This was my nursery. This shall be my tomb.

The monsters come less often now and, when they do, they usually just stand at the wardrobe door and mock me. Most are voiceless and merely roll their eyes about and dance obscenely. Tonight, however, a familiar form comes to break the silent tradition of my torture. My first devil. Poison drips from every part of his body and his words are poison, too. He laughs at my impotence as he tells me of the helpless terror of sleeping children in a whole world full of wardrobes and bedrooms and beds. He tells me to leave, says the girl is never returning. "Relic", he calls me. "Useless". "Forgotten". With a cackle he turns and disappears back into the wardrobe.

And he leaves the door open behind him.

As I gaze at the opening, I feel a stirring in my thinning blood, an ancient and familiar calling in my brittle bones. Purpose. I drag myself up. My neglected muscles strain with the effort, but I feel them grow stronger with each step toward my goal. With a hunger for demonic flesh welling up within me, and a thousand other hungers besides, I leave my nursery of dust and cobwebs and I follow the monster into the wardrobe.

WHAT WE FOUND AMONG THE DUNES

ELISHA FROUDE WAS my best friend and that wintry weekend it was her turn to play host at our regular sleep-over. After school on Friday we boarded the bus—me with my sleeping-bag and overnight luggage—and headed out of town to Elisha's family's farm.

Elisha's father, Bill, decided he wanted to go fishing and, seeing her mother was at work (she was a nurse at the local hospital) he bundled us into the back of his truck and brought us along with him to the beach. We sat in the bed of the truck underneath an itchy grey blanket and giggled while we nibbled furtively at the fresh Anzac biscuits we had stolen from the pantry.

When we arrived at the beach Mr Froude collected his rod and tackle and immediately headed for the shore, giving us the one directive - "Don't wander off too far."

If it had been my own father, he would have told us not to wander off at all and would have made sure he kept an eagle-eye on the both of us, but Bill Froude's parenting style was much more relaxed. I was giddy at the prospect of the unaccustomed freedom.

The beach was all but deserted, which wasn't entirely surprising. It was a cold, miserable day, after all, and the wind whipped the sand about us, stinging my bare legs. I wrapped a towel around my waist to try and protect myself.

Elisha was clutching a large plastic bucket. "Let's look for shells," she suggested, and I agreed. It certainly wasn't a day for swimming. Rather than heading towards the shoreline, Elisha led me towards the dunes at the far end of the beach. There were fewer shells here, but at least we would avoid the icy, churning waves. We wandered through those sandy mounds, gradually adding little treasures to our collection as we made our progress.

Putting down her bucket at the base of the largest dune Elisha declared, “Let’s race to the top!”, then immediately began her ascent. Letting out a squeal of protest, I quickly scrambled after her. The further we climbed up the dune, the deeper and deeper our legs sank into the sand until, panting from the exertion and only half-way up, we gave up the race.

Looking down at our progress, I felt a little flutter of anxiety, “We’re so high up!” I moaned but Elisha, unperturbed, merely laughed. She dug her legs out of the sand and sat down on her backside. Using her arms, she launched herself forward and began to slide down the dune. I soon followed suit, descending feet first and screaming the whole way.

This became our new game and I lost track of the number of times we climbed the steep slopes of the dunes and slid back down. Reaching the foot of one of the dunes, the heel of my foot struck something hard just below the surface of the sand. I let out a cry, more of surprise than pain, and stopped to dig frantically at the sand uncovering a long, white bone.

"Ellie!" I called to my friend.

"What is it?" she called as she approached, and I gestured wordlessly at the bone. Elisha squatted in the sand beside me and examined my discovery for one long moment before confirming, "It's a bone."

"Yes, but what kind of bone?" I asked but she did not respond. "A dog?" I added.

"It's way too big to be a dog bone!" Elisha scoffed. She looked up at me then, her eyes bright, "Maybe it's a dinosaur bone!"

"M-ayyyyybe" I allowed, then reached out to stroke the bone, marvelling at its glassy-smooth surface. I looked about us and noted for the first time the dry scrubland that lay directly behind the dunes. "Could it be a kangaroo bone?" I offered and Elisha nodded sagely, "Could be. Could be."

After a few more moments of mutual contemplation, Elisha eventually declared, "Probably it's a horse's bone."

"It's way more interesting than the

shells!" I said, and the two of us looked at each-other. Our eyes locked and, in a moment of perfect understanding, we picked up Elisha's bucket together and up-ended it, depositing our meagre collection of shells onto the sand before reverently placing the bone in their place.

"There's another one!" Elisha cried in delight and I followed her gaze. Sure enough, no more than three metres away from us, another roughly cylindrical object jutted out of the sand.

We began to pick our way around the base of that sand dune, uncovering more and more bones the longer we looked. Some, like the first we uncovered, were sitting atop the sand or just below it, but as we dug deeper we uncovered whole caches of bones in different sizes and shapes all jumbled together, all forming a ring around the base of that particular dune.

And then we found the skull.

It really was a horse, after all, or something like a horse anyway. It's large, perfectly formed and sun-bleached skull had a broad forehead that sloped gradually into a long muzzle. Right at the top of the muzzle a sharp outcrop of bone jutted forward marking, I supposed, the bridge of its nose. *Yes, it really must be a horse*, I thought. *Except horses aren't supposed to have sharp teeth, are they?*

The teeth right to the very front of the skull were wide and flat and generally what I expected a horse's teeth to look like, not that I'd ever thought about it before. Directly behind them, however, set a little further back further in the jaw, were two long curved teeth. They were like fangs. It looked wrong to me but being a townie, I looked to Elisha for confirmation. My friend was squatting down beside the skull, frowning as she trailed one finger lazily around its empty eye-socket. I held my breath. Finally, Elisha's features broke into a grin and she patted the forehead of the skull familiarly. "Good horsy!" she declared. I breathed.

We added the skull to the top of our bucket of bones and regarded our collection with satisfaction. Then, a thought occurred to me, "Will your Dad let us keep them?"

The smile faded from Elisha's face. She kicked fiercely at the sand and pouted. I untied the towel from my waist and draped it delicately over the bucket. "There!" I announced, "Now your dad will just think it's full of shells." but Elisha was unconvinced.

"What if he asks why it has a towel over it?" she asked.

"We could tell him we don't want to get sand in the back of the truck?" I suggested. At this, we both looked down at our sand-encrusted legs and feet. It was obvious that this excuse wouldn't work. "Maybe we could say we don't want the wind to blow them away?" Elisha offered, but even she seemed unconvinced.

In the end, it didn't really matter as the fishing had been bad and Elisha's dad was in no mood for conversation. He spoke little more than a grunt as he boosted us each up and into the bed of the truck and did not even give the bucket a second glance.

When we got back to the farm, Elisha and I took our treasure straight to her treehouse, where we knew we would not be disturbed. We spread the towel out on the floor and then began to delicately lay out each of the bones. I'll never forget the way the usually exuberant Elisha handled each specimen with a gentleness that bordered on reverence. It did not strike me as odd at the time that each bone was complete and undamaged, and each an almost-radiant white.

Wordlessly, we started trying to arrange the bones into some sort of order. It was like trying to complete a jigsaw puzzle without aid of the picture on the box and, as with any jigsaw puzzle, after ten minutes or so I began to get bored. "Can we go back inside and watch 'The Last Unicorn' now?" I asked Elisha, but my friend didn't respond. Instead she just rocked back on her heels, clutching her knees to her chest and staring fixedly at the pile that lay on the treehouse floor. "We're almost finished," I heard her mutter under her breath. I looked sceptically at the jumble of bones spread out between us. "Ellie?" I pressed and this time she did look up at me, glaring as she snapped, "What?!"

I was taken aback by her tone, but just replied, "It's late. You said we could watch a movie and have ice-cream." Elisha's face immediately softened, "Oh, yeah! Let's do that." She stood up, brushing some stray grains of sand off her knobbly knees. "We can finish this later," she said, casting a strangely longing glance back to the pile of bones.

*

Waking that night to the unfamiliar ceiling of Elisha's bedroom, I felt a moment of panic before remembering where I was.

Even after I recognised my surroundings I still felt faintly uneasy. "Ellie, are you awake?" I asked in a stage whisper and then, when I received no response, a little louder, "Elisha!"

In the silence that followed I could hear my own heartbeat hammering in my ears. Wriggling free of my sleeping-bag, I sat up and strained to see over the edge of my friend's bed. It was empty.

This was nothing unusual, I told myself. Elisha must have gotten up to go to the toilet or get a glass of water. When fifteen minutes passed and she still had not returned my anxiety got the better of me and, stuffing my feet into my fuzzy slippers, I crept out into the hallway.

I tip-toed as quietly as I could manage past Elisha's parents' room, certain I would get into trouble if I woke them up. The bathroom light was out, but I opened the door just to be sure, "Elisha," I whispered into the darkness, but the only response was the steady drip-drip of a leaky faucet. I approached the sink and tightened the tap firmly before slipping back out into the hallway.

The kitchen was likewise abandoned. I even checked the walk-in pantry in case Elisha had snuck in for a midnight snack, but the little room with its neatly stocked shelves gave no indication of my friend's presence.

I was stumped, and more than a little nervous. I wondered if Elisha could have been playing a prank on me–she had a wicked sense of humour, after all. But this didn't feel right. Elisha was more scared of her parents than I was, so why would she sneak around in middle of the night when we were supposed to be in bed with the lights out?

Briefly, I considered knocking on her parents' bedroom door and telling them Elisha was missing, but the fear of punishment held me back. I stood awkwardly and indecisively in the middle of the kitchen floor. Should I just go back to bed and hope Elisha came back on her own? I had almost decided to do just that when a thought occurred to me–the treehouse.

Surely if Elisha was hiding that

would be the obvious place to look? Perhaps she was waiting for me, betting that I would not be brave enough to join her. I felt offended at this thought and, with a new resolve, I strode up to the door leading from the kitchen into the back yard and stepped out onto the veranda.

It was dark outside. Much darker than it ever was at my own house in town. At first, I could see nothing apart from the scattering of stars and the thin sliver of moon above. Eventually, as my eyes adjusted, I could just barely make out the silhouette of Elisha's treehouse, the moonlight glinting off its corrugated-iron roof. I started to make my way towards the treehouse, but halfway across the lawn I noticed that, aside from the reflected moonlight, the treehouse was emitting its own faint glow from somewhere within. From the window and doorway, I saw flickering yellow lights.

Buzzing with a potent blend of fear and excitement, I made my faltering way up the rickety ladder. From the ground I could hear a faint whispering and, assuming it was Elisha, felt reassured. I couldn't tell who she was talking to, but if Elisha was talking to them they couldn't be that dangerous.

Hoisting myself through the doorway of the treehouse I was confronted with the sight of Elisha standing in the middle of the space, her back facing towards me and her head hanging low. I noticed, too, the white taper candles burning on the upturned milk-crate Elisha used as a table. I couldn't see anyone else, nor could I make out what Elisha was saying.

"Elisha?" I asked, and my voice cracked a little bit. She spun around, clutching one of the plain white candles in a tightly bunched fist. Its glow cast shadows that sharpened her features; her chin appeared pointed, her cheeks hollow, her eyes sunken. Her mouth was set in a manic grin, like I was staring at a skull. I was so startled I stumbled backwards and had to grab the doorframe with both hands to steady myself.

"I'm almost finished!" she hissed below her breath, gesturing to the floor. It didn't look 'almost finished' to me. What I saw was part of a ribcage and what might have been a shoulder. I looked back at Elisha and saw that she was gazing at me expectantly, her eyes fever-bright in the candlelight. She was waiting for me to say something—to praise her work—but all I could think about was Elisha's parents lying in their bed–still asleep, perhaps, but for how long?

“Let's go back to bed,” I pleaded, tugging at my friend's pyjama sleeve. “Before we get in trouble.”

The smile faded from Elisha's face. I expected her to resist, but instead she just nodded solemnly and, blowing out the candles, allowed me to lead her down the ladder and back into the house.

*

Elisha was not at school the following Monday and I spent my time hanging out with my other best friend, Keeley. We played together at lunch time and we giggled and talked about whatever it was we were interested in at the time. Cartoons, maybe? Or books, even. All I really remember is that it was the last time for quite a while that things felt normal.

Elisha returned to school the next day, though she was unusually subdued. When I eventually got a chance to talk to her she explained that her father had fallen suddenly ill and that her mother had kept her and her brother home under suspicion that they may have the same virus. Certainly, Elisha did not look well to me. She was all slouched over and there were dark rings under her eyes. Her voice, too, was uncharacteristically flat and she seemed reluctant to look me in the eye when she spoke. I must confess, I ignored her for most of the day until lunch time when, seeing her lingering by the lockers after grabbing her lunch and thinking she looked lonely I approached her and asked how she was going with the bones. At the question, Elisha immediately brightened. "Great!" she chirped, a gleam in her previously dull eyes. "I'm almost finished! I just need a little help."

I panicked at this and began formulating in my head excuses for why I couldn't come over to her place, but it didn't matter in the end because she bid me a flippant, "Seeya!" then headed off in the direction of the school library.

Elisha borrowed every book the library had on horses. She had never been much of a reader and I remember later asking the school librarian if she thought this was odd. She replied, "I just assumed she wanted to look at the pictures."

She was right, in a way. In class that afternoon I looked over at Elisha's seat to find her staring at her lap where, hidden by her desk, she had laid one of the books out. It was open at a double page spread of a horse's skeletal structure and she was tracing it with one finger, silently mouthing words as she went.

Elisha's attendance over the next few weeks of school became sporadic, at best. When she did show up, she was often late and always looked tired and wan. Always a slight girl, Elisha began to look worn and haggard. With her stooped posture and hollow cheeks she looked less like a little girl and more like a frail old lady.

Rumours started to spread around the school about Elisha and her family. That her father's illness was getting worse and her mother had to leave her job to take care of him. That her older brother, who went to the high school further along the road, was getting into trouble at school, skipping classes and picking fights.

Whenever I spoke to her, Elisha

would not comment on this gossip, waving it aside whenever I brought it up. All she was interested in was those bones. Every time I spoke to her she would state with increasing conviction that, "I'm almost finished!" It was all she could talk about, expanding her vocabulary to include strange new words I didn't recognise like 'carpus' and 'phalanges'. I found her obsession both creepy and boring and, I am ashamed to say, I began avoiding her. This wasn't too difficult, given her infrequent appearances at school.

In a few weeks, news reached the playground that Adrian, Elisha's brother, had been expelled from school. This sparked further rumours about the Froude family. Someone said they had heard their parents say that Bill Froude's extended illness had made him cruel. Although I didn't actively spread these stories, I didn't speak out against them, either. When I eventually heard rumours that Elisha's parents were getting divorced and that Adrian and Elisha would be moving with their mother to Perth, I even began to wonder if the rumours may actually be true.

*

One day, in the middle of summer, Elisha returned to school after being absent for several weeks. She was even thinner than before, but there was a spring in her step that had been missing for several months and she smiled broadly at me when she entered the classroom, making me flush with shame as I thought of all the rumours I had listened to about her and her family.

At recess, Elisha accosted me by the lockers and pulled me into an empty classroom. She was literally quaking with excitement as she revealed to me in a conspiratorial whisper, "I'm finished!"

Given how long it had been since we last spoke, it took several seconds for the meaning of Elisha's words to penetrate.

"The bones?' I asked her.

"The *skeleton*," she corrected. "It's finished now and it's something really special. I can't wait to show you. Do you want to come over this Friday?"

I most certainly did not. Although a part of me was curious about what Elisha had finally managed to construct from our find, I could not forget all the rumours about her family. It seemed to me that the Froude household would not be a fun place to visit any more. Besides, I felt like Elisha and I had drifted apart over the last few months.

Elisha was waiting for a response, her hands clasped together in a pleading gesture.

"Yes," I eventually replied. What else could I say?

Friday soon arrived and Elisha had been strangely silent on her favourite topic. I was still going to spend the night at her place, but there was no talk of bones or skeletons. All day, however, Elisha had virtually been vibrating with barely suppressed excitement.

When we arrived at Elisha's place after school her father was mercifully absent. I did not ask where he was.

It seemed almost like things were back to how they had been before we went digging around the sand dunes. We spent the afternoon playing Adrian's Super Nintendo while he was out riding his dirt bike on some distant part of the Froude property.

For dinner we had chicken pie and dessert was freshly baked scones with lashings of cream and jam.

We watched TV until, to my relief, Elisha's mother announced that it was time for us to go to bed.

Despite the relief, I slept uneasily that night, still feeling that something was not quite right. I was still awake, therefore, when Elisha whispered from her bed, “It's time to go”.

Fear ran through me like an electric current and I considered pretending to be asleep, but Elisha was propped on her side now and had seen my wide-open eyes staring at the ceiling.

“Let's go!” she hissed impatiently, swinging her legs over the edge of the bed and prodding at me with a foot. Meekly, I complied.

We tip-toed down the corridor, Elisha expertly navigating around the squeaky floorboards and I struggling to mimic her steps in the dark. When we got to the kitchen Elisha pulled out a waxy stub of a candle and lit it, tucking the box of matches into the waistband of her pyjamas. I could see a torch lying in the drawer right next to where the candle had been and I wondered why Elisha had not taken this instead, but I was too afraid of making a noise to actually ask her.

Together we slipped out of the kitchen door and crept towards Elisha's treehouse. When we climbed the ladder I wondered what Elisha would do with the candle, but she just placed it between her teeth, the flame flickering dangerously close to her cheek. When we reached the top, I saw why Elisha had not taken the flashlight. The entire inside of the tree house was crammed with a multitude of candles, which Elisha now went and lit one by one. They formed a perimeter around a bare space in the centre of the floor. I did not want to look at what was in the middle.

Once Elisha had finished, she reached out her free hand towards me, “Come and see!” she urged quietly but insistently. Reluctantly, I stepped over the ring of candles and into the centre of the treehouse.

I stood staring at the display at my feet for some time before looking back to Elisha, seeking an explanation.

“I think it's a unicorn!” she whispered gleefully.

I looked again at the bones. The torso was roughly laid out in a shape that could have been read as that of a horse. The neck, though...

The neck was too long, longer than a camel's, perhaps even as long as a giraffe's. Instead of laying the neck out in a straight column, however, Elisha had for some reason decided to snake the vertebrae out in a series of serpentine coils.

The hooves of the beast were small and cloven (how had I not noticed this when we dug them up?) and the tail, like the neck, was long and twisted.

Near the top of the skull Elisha had placed a bone I did not recognise at all. It was long and curved like a sickle, so that it seemed almost like its pointed tip would have pierced the back of the beast's head.

I stared down for some time at that skull with its curved horn and the mouth full of incongruously sharp teeth. I gazed into those empty eye sockets and swear for a moment I saw something glow within them. My stomach lurched with dread.

I do not remember climbing out of the treehouse. I do not remember running back inside. All I remember was locking myself in the bathroom and sobbing so hard and so loud that it got Elisha's mother out of bed.

When she asked what was wrong,

I didn't answer at first, then I replied that I felt sick, "I want to go home!" I choked out between sobs.

When my father drove over to pick me up Elisha's mother was hovering around me–anxious and full of apologies. Elisha was somewhere in the background, but I couldn't bring myself to look at her, not even when my father guided me gingerly out the front door and towards the car.

*

I was not surprised, at first, when Elisha didn't show up at school on Monday. I had been thinking all weekend about what I would say when I saw her and had decided that I would not bring up Friday's events at all and that if she tried to talk to me about skeletons or mythical beasts I would just walk away.

Our teacher, the soft-spoken Miss Morris, looked uncharacteristically grim when she greeted the class that morning. "Alright, children, I have some bad news," she said in her breathy voice. "You may have noticed that Elisha Froude is not in class this morning—" Many had not noticed. This was not unusual, after all. "I'm very sorry to say that there's been a death in her family."

My chest tightened as I thought of Elisha's father's absence on Friday.

"—Elisha's brother Adrian came off his motorbike when he was riding on the weekend. He hadn't been wearing his helmet and the doctors weren't able to save him."

Adrian? I felt the blood drain out of my face. How could it be? I had just seen him on Friday. I had eaten my dinner opposite him at their kitchen table. How could he be dead?

"—Elisha will not be at school for a while—" Miss Morris continued, her voice growing faint and tremulous. I barely took in any more of what she said, though I remember her finishing by tearfully pleading with the class, "So please, children, promise me you'll always wear your helmets when you go riding, even if it's just a push-bike."

I couldn't focus on my schoolwork that day, or for the rest of the week, really. It didn't seem fair, didn't even seem possible, that one family should go through so much, and in such a short space of time. It had all started when Elisha and I brought home those wretched bones. I shuddered at the memory of that warped skeleton lying on the floor of Elisha's treehouse, surrounded by candles like a relic in some shrine.

I cursed the day we went to the beach and cursed the very dunes for what we found buried there. Most of all I cursed myself for ever stumbling upon that first shaft of bone.

Lying in bed one night, I decided that something would have to be done. I would go to Elisha's place, sneak into the treehouse, take the bones and bury them somewhere far away or, better yet, take a hammer and smash them into powder for the hot, dry winds to carry where they would.

I felt a little better now that I had a kind of plan in place. Now I just had to wait for an opportunity to visit Elisha. *Perhaps I can ask Mum and Dad if we can bring Mrs Froude some flowers tomorrow?*

I never had my opportunity. When I woke up the next morning, I found my parents sitting silently at the dining-room table–a pot of hot tea steaming between them. My mother looked up when I entered the room. She had been crying.

My father walked over to me and

hugged me tight. “I'm so sorry, kiddo,” he whispered.

“What's wrong?” I asked, my voice beginning to break. I already knew what was wrong or, rather, who it had happened to.

“There's been a fire...at Elisha's place. Her mother and her were both asleep when it started and... I’m so sorry... they didn't survive.”

My mother let out a tiny sob. I felt like someone had dropped a lump of ice right in my belly.

I was quiet for some time. What was there to say? My father filled in the silence with more details of the events: “The house was weatherboard and it's been so hot and dry...” I only half listened.

One question did, however, finally come to mind, “What about Mr Froude?”

There was a pause before my father, his voice tense, said, “They don't know where Bill is. The police are still looking for him.” The significance of this statement was lost on me at the time.

I asked my parents if I could go back to the Froude farm–told them I wanted to say goodbye. They exchanged a meaningful look when I made this request, then gently tried to discourage me. When I wouldn't relent it was my mother who eventually told me that there was no point going back to the farm. There was nothing left after the fire. Not even bones.

THE NEW GIRL

I'M NOT SURE, even now, what possessed me to put my hand up.

Whenever a new student joined the class it would always go the same way–if she looked likely enough, the popular girls would have first dibs on her. If they weren't interested, then the teacher's pet, eager to please, would be next to volunteer. Few other people would ever be expected to take on this duty, and certainly not someone as far to the fringe as I was.

This time, however, when the new girl stood at the front of the class and the teacher (Mr O'Brien, because it was Social Studies) asked who would like to take her under their wing there was an awkward silence. People shuffled in their seats. Someone coughed. Then, slowly but deliberately, I raised my hand.

Mr O'Brien frowned as he looked in my direction,

"Haley?" he said, a little sceptically. The people in the front of the classroom swivelled around in their desks to look at me. I could feel myself shrink beneath the weight of their collective gaze, but I kept my hand resolutely aloft.

"She can sit here," I said, referring to the empty desk beside me (there was always an empty desk beside me). Mr O'Brien cast his eyes over the rest of the class then, as though seeking an alternative. When none were forthcoming, he merely shrugged and then gestured with his hand for the new girl to join me.

The new girl approached the desk beside me, and I watched out of the corner of my eye as, with a poise that struck me as uncharacteristic of a 17-year-old girl, she lowered herself into the chair.

“Thank you,” she whispered to me as Mr O'Brien resumed his lecturing.

“No worries,” I muttered, feeling my face flush pink.

What can I tell you about the new girl? She was tall and skinny. So skinny, in fact, that one might think her to be frail (though I later learnt this was far from the truth). Her lips, too, were thin and I had the feeling that there must have been something wrong with her teeth, for she never smiled and spoke only in hissing whispers through barely parted lips. Her fine hair was a very fair shade of blonde and it hung dead-straight at about shoulder-length.

Oh, but her eyes were bright green all flecked with brown freckles. Cold and unflinching they seemed to strip you bare as soon as she lay them on you. There was nothing you could hide from eyes like that.

And, now that I think of it more, it really must have been the eyes that did it. From the very first moment she turned those smouldering orbs upon me I belonged to her and I didn’t really have a choice in anything else that followed. I didn’t have a choice.

*

I'm sure that anyone who saw us could not have imagined a more unlikely pair: she tall and elegant, possessed of a confidence and dignity that shamed most adults and I, short (and, frankly, rather dumpy) and so awkward I had been given up by most as a lost cause. The weirdo and the new girl.

When I asked her what country she was from she insisted that her family had always lived in Australia, but a part of me remained sceptical. To my ear her voice had the slow, deliberate precision of someone who spoke English as a second language. Her complexion, too, set her apart–her skin so pale it was transparent in places.

Once we became friends (which is to say, almost immediately) I used to sleep over at her place quite frequently. Once a fortnight, almost. The first time she invited me around I was so nervous. It was a Friday and I brought my sleeping bag to school so we could take the bus straight back to her place in the afternoon. She sat silently for the entire trip and, sitting beside her, I felt all tingly with anticipation. I stared intently out of the window, focusing my gaze on nothing in particular and wondering about... well, everything really. What would her house look like? Would her parents be friendly? What would we have for dinner?

I was so rapt in my speculations that when she reached out and squeezed my hand I just about jumped out of my skin. "This is our stop." she whispered, and I hastily scraped up my backpack and sleeping bag and scrambled off the bus behind her, mumbling a quick thanks to the bus driver as he closed the door behind me.

As we trudged off towards her house the new girl explained that, even though her family weren't farmers, they always preferred to live out of town. "The rent is cheaper." she explained, "And, besides, we like the peace and quiet, especially considering my parents do shift work."

'Peace and quiet' was right. When we arrived at her house I was struck by what seemed like a complete lack of ambient noise. I had always lived in the middle of town and had little experience of what you might call, 'real country living'. I had always assumed that living on a farm would be quieter but shouldn't there have been *some* noise?

Her house, which was set about 100 metres back from the road on a one hectare property, was a moderately-sized weatherboard structure. The inside—neat and minimalist—was completely different from the chaotic eclecticism of my own family home.

The new girl gave me a quick tour of the home, skipping her parents' room as her mother was sleeping.

The tour terminated in her bedroom at the far side of the house where she cast off her backpack and encouraged me to do the same. I scanned the room and noted that the walls were bare but for a dog-eared poster of a rock band that had split up some years ago.

My eyes rested on the large queen single bed (her bed, I thought to myself with a little thrill) in the centre of the room. A little shyly I went and sat on the edge of the bed while she showed me her small collection of colourful glass perfume bottles, which were arranged attractively on a white veneer dressing table–much like the one in my own bedroom.

It was fascinating just watching

her handle the bottles–picking each up delicately, almost reverently, and turning them this way and that in her hands so that they caught the afternoon light that crept in through the Venetian blinds of her window. I watched her long, white fingers glide smoothly over the curves and bulges of the bottles and shivered a little.

Later on, we watched some movies. I had brought along one of my favourite films, 'Poltergeist', which she had told me previously she had never seen. For the entire length of the movie I kept stealing sideways glances at her looking for signs of fear but, although she seemed to be watching the film with intense concentration, I never once saw her flinch.

It was late when the new girl finally peeled herself off the couch and led the way back to her bedroom. I went to unfurl my sleeping bag when she spoke from behind me, so softly that I first thought I had imagined it, "It's cold," she said. "Come sleep in the bed with me."

I froze. Surely, I had misheard her? Slowly, pulse thundering in my ears, I turned towards the bed, where I saw that the new girl had already slipped beneath the covers. Our eyes met and, holding my gaze, she shuffled over to the far side, making room. With just a moment's hesitation I awkwardly clambered in beside her, thanking God for the darkness that hid my scarlet cheeks.

I rolled onto my side so that I faced the edge of the bed and lay there stiffly. I could sense her lying behind me. I could have reached back and touched her if I wanted. Of course, I did want to... but I contented myself with the knowledge of her proximity.

Suddenly, I felt something that made me catch my breath–a fingernail running up my back, tracing my spine through my nightie. I shivered as the new girl, wordlessly, trailed a finger upwards until it met the nape of my neck. Once there, she began, oh so softly, to run her fingers through my hair.

From the darkness behind me she spoke in that low susurration that made every sentence she uttered sound like a prayer. "Do you believe in ghosts?" she asked, and I replied, "Yes," without even thinking about it. So quickly did I make my answer that it almost took me by surprise. Afraid of seeming naive, I was about to clarify when she re-joined, “Me too.” And so I remained silent.

Eventually, with the new girl’s fingers still tangled in my hair, I fell asleep.

*

I always felt particularly pious after Ash Wednesday mass. Something about having that symbol of faith on my person—the cross smeared across the forehead in ash—seemed to make the whole thing more tangible somehow.

Back in primary school we had borne these marks as a kind of status symbol. There would be something of a competition to see whose cross lasted the longest. In our teens, now, most would wash the marks of their foreheads as soon as we returned to school. This always seemed disrespectful to me—sacrilegious, in fact—so I left mine untouched, a point that always drew my peers’ scorn.

She didn’t wash hers off either. Walking through the playground with her I felt, for the first time since primary school, proud of the mark. It was another thing that linked me to her.

I felt like a gang member, or a branded slave.

We slipped behind the PE shed to talk, as we did most lunchtimes. Sitting with our backs against the corrugated iron we spoke in hushed tones of the usual things–problems with homework, what we thought of our classmates and teachers, last night's episode of 'Buffy'. I was idly picking at a patch of grass beside me when all of a sudden, I felt her hand—pale and cool like marble—rest on my own.

My glance darted up to her face, but she was just staring straight ahead, her face as smooth and expressionless as a wax mask–the only blemish on those perfect features the smudged cross on her forehead. We sat frozen like that for some time before she finally broke the silence.

"Do you believe in angels?" she asked me. This time I did stop to consider things. I remembered the medallion my parents placed over my bed as a child depicting a guardian angel watching over a small girl and boy. I thought, too, of my favourite book to browse in the school library: 'An Encyclopaedia of Angels (Including the Fallen Angels)'. I gazed at the new girl's besmirched forehead and thought of the twin mark on my own face.

"Yes?" I said, a little cautiously.

It may have just been my imagination, but I thought I saw the corners of her mouth twitch. Suddenly, she clutched my hand so hard I gasped. Turning to me, she murmured, "Me too," then bent down and pressed her taut lips firmly, almost aggressively, against my own.

As we sat there, lips joined in that oddly chaste kiss (she didn't open her mouth or offer her tongue) I found myself thinking with a kind of awe, "I really do believe in angels."

*

During the Christmas holidays my parents agreed to let me stay over at her place for five whole nights. They were a little reluctant when the proposition was raised. They had only ever spoken to the new girl's parents over the phone and had never actually met them (neither had I, for that matter, because they were always either asleep or at work). They were relieved, though, that I finally seemed to have made a friend and so eventually acquiesced.

The sleep-over went much the same as any of the others we had shared. We watched movies, ate junk food and talked. We even dabbled with a makeshift Ouija board I had constructed covertly during art class, but the spirits did not deign to acknowledge our efforts. When it got so late that it was early, we headed back to her bedroom and slipped between the sheets together.

Mostly we just slept, but occasionally she would braid my hair or stroke at my cheek with dainty fingers. Sometimes she even permitted me to caress her reclining form or even to kiss her. She never spoke at these times, just sighed softly as I pressed my lips to her smooth neck or her high cheekbones or her fluttering eyelids.

On the third night of my visit we stayed up particularly late watching a succession of Hammer films about satanic cults (I don't remember any of the titles and the details of the movies themselves are all blurred together in my recollection).

When we eventually did make it to bed, we lay face to face. The new girl's steady, rhythmic breathing was tickling my nose and I thought she must already have fallen asleep but then—her thin lips so close they brushed against mine—she whispered, "Do you believe in demons?"

I took longer to answer this question than I had her previous ones. Angels were a part of my theology, after all, and everyone believed in ghosts (everyone I knew, anyway) but demons?

I tried to avoid the question—leaning in and pressing my lips to hers—but she gently pushed me away and just repeated her question, "Do you believe in demons?"

Thwarted, I gave over to considering the question seriously. I'd never really given the topic of demonology much thought, but was it really any stranger than the other beliefs I held? If I believed in angels, didn't I have to believe in demons as their natural counterpoint?

After a moment more of hesitation I eventually conceded that, yes, I did believe in demons. I waited, then, for her usual response–only half-listening as I trailed one index finger down the slope of her shoulder and along her delicate collarbone. But she didn't give her usual response. Not this time.

Instead, she rolled onto her back

and, staring at the ceiling, she spoke, "The old man next door is a demon."

A shiver, not entirely unpleasant, ran down my spine. I asked her what she meant and in her characteristically detached tone she recounted the whole sad, strange tale of the demon that had dogged her family for years:

"I don't know how or why it started and neither do my parents... or so they tell me, anyway. All I know is that, for as long as I can remember, this demon has been following me and my family. Everywhere we go he appears and terrorises us until, eventually, we have to move. But it doesn't seem to matter how far or how often we move. He always finds us eventually.

"It always starts the same way—with the dreams. Whenever we get settled in a new place, anywhere from a week to a few of months after we move, I start having these dreams. Awful, bloody dreams. Nightmares, really. I'm running through some bushland. I do not know where, exactly. It is night-time and it is eerily quiet. The only sound is the dry leaves crunching under my feet and the sound of my own heartbeat hammering in my ears. Ahead of me I see a figure, a man, and I move towards him–seeking help. As I approach, I can see that he is very old and very frail. Shrivelled up. He is bent over as though with pain or fatigue. Then, I realise that something is not right. He looks like an old man, but he is not. He opens his mouth and it is too big, filled with too many teeth. The teeth are narrow and pointed and dripping with blood. He looks at me and his eyes are like a goat's. I freeze under that gaze. I cannot move at all. But then my eyes are drawn downward to a huddled shape at the demon's feet. I realise with dread certainty that it is a dead body. With his clawed feet the demon rolls the corpse over so that I can see its face. My face. At that point I always wake up."

"That's...pretty creepy." I replied.

"That is just the beginning." she whispered.

She told me, then, of the myriad misfortunes with which her family had been beset–missing objects, plagues of insects, blighted crops and gardens, dead livestock, mutilated pets. The demon would lay tragedy after tragedy upon their doorstep in ever escalating degrees until eventually, inevitably, they would be forced to move again...

only for the whole cycle to repeat itself in their new setting.

It was then that she delivered the final, devastating point, "My parents have not been home for days. I thought that if I just waited, if I pretended that everything was normal, then maybe they would come back. But he has taken them. I know it. And I think he means to take me next."

"No!" I cried, clutching desperately at her hand like a frightened child.

"He will come for me, will kill me probably. Unless..."

Her voice trailed off and I saw her eyes grow misty.

"'Unless' what?" I implored, squeezing her hand.

"Unless we get to him, first."

"What?!" I cried, letting go of the new girl's hand in my alarm.

"You and I, we could do it. We could sneak right into the demon's lair and banish him back to whatever circle of hell he came from."

"I... I don't know." I stammered. "Isn't there something else we could do? The police—"

"—The police will not believe a word of this," she reasoned. "They will think it is some kind of prank. By the time we managed to convince them… convince anyone… of our story, it will be too late for me."

Suddenly, she swung the long stems of her legs out of the bed and stood up. "You and I, we can end this. Tonight. Now."

"O-okay," I stammered, sitting up and shuffling to the edge of the bed. "Just let me put some clothes on and—"

"Now," she insisted firmly. "We do it now or we will never do it." And with that she headed out the door, clad only in her silk pyjamas. I barely had time to stuff my feet into my moccasins as I stumbled after her.

The moon was full and bright that night, the grass all wet with dew. The new girl glided through the darkness like a sliver of starlight–pale and almost luminous.

We decided that it was best to approach his house from the back, and to get there we had to pick our way through the empty and overgrown paddocks that separated their two properties.

While I scrambled clumsily over the wire fences, she came at each barrier at a run and vaulted over with effortless, skeletal grace. "She's like a deer," I thought to myself, struck by the sight of her tense, wiry figure leaping in the moonlight. "Like some wild gazelle."

It's a bit of a fallacy what they say about no one in the country locking their doors but, fortunately for us, in this case it proved true. We opened the back door without obstacle and slipped into the darkened house like shadows.

There were no curtains on any of the windows and the light streaming in from the full moon was enough for us to make out the essential elements of our surroundings. We had entered a laundry—a narrow space occupied by a large, deep sink and the obtrusive bulk of an old washing-machine. We crept past these and through an open door into the cramped kitchen.

Here, the new girl paused. I halted also and watched closely as she daintily tip-toed up to the bench and opened the top drawer. "What is she doing?" I wondered, but not for long, as she swiftly drew out a sharp chopping knife and examined it in the moonlight. She turned and wordlessly motioned for me to join her. She gestured at the open drawer and, hand shaking, I reached in and grabbed another knife–smaller than hers. Thinner, but no less sharp. "Probably for filleting fish" I thought irrelevantly. Thus armed, we resumed our stealthy progress.

Attached to the kitchen was a small dining area and adjacent to this was a door leading to what must have been the living room. I could not suppress a gasp as we entered this room. Lining the walls was a startling array of bladed weapons and tools–sickles, scimitars and scythes. Knives of every shape and size. As we passed by, I thought, briefly, of exchanging my kitchen blade for one of the more ornate daggers on the wall, but I had made my choice.

We were less than halfway across the room when the light flicked on. "Who's there?" demanded a high, querulous voice.

The old man was just as the new girl had described him–a gaunt, stooping figure. A dried-up, raisin of a man. *Not a man*, I had to remind myself. *Not really*.

The old man—the demon—rolled his rheumy eyes this way and that in their sunken sockets, taking in the entirety of the scene before coming to rest on the new girl. "It's you!" the demon cried (and what was that odd tone that entered his voice? Indignation? Loathing? Fear?)

"It is I," the new girl confirmed in her calm monotone, blinking impassively.

The old man lurched forward, reaching out with both arms as though to throttle her. Acting on instincts I didn't know I had, I dropped my knife and barrelled into the man, head-butting him in the gut and knocking him to the ground, where he lay sprawled on his back.

Panting, I fell to my knees by his head and hooked my arms under his armpits, restraining him. I was not very strong, but he was so frail that I didn't have to be.

I am surprised by how quickly the whole thing passed. One minute he was thrashing about in my grasp–spitting and swearing–and then the new girl, in one fluid movement, plunged the knife deep into his throat. The demon's eyes widened and there was a wet gurgling noise as the blood (so much blood) bubbled and surged out of him. It ran off his neck and pooled on the carpet–spreading out and staining the hem of my nightie, the bare soles of the new girl's feet.

And, just like that, it was done. The demon, defeated, lay still in a pool of his own blood. It was hard to believe that I, that we, had done this great and terrible thing. Together. We had killed the demon together and, as his foul blood seeped further into our night-clothes and stained our skin, I knew that in this act we had forged a bond that would never be broken.

Elated, exhilarated, I looked up at the new girl and grinned. And, for the first time ever...

...She smiled back at me

About the Author

Katherine Kitchener is an Australian-based horror author who loves short stories, sad songs, scary games, sweet treats and little ponies. You can find her on Twitter as "@Spookatherine".

About the Illustrator

Carlos Sánchez goes by the nick "Dood" online. He is an illustrator, comic artist and sometimes writer who loves horror, fantasy and sci-fi, in that order. You can find him on twitter as "@ CSPStuff" or as "ddoodler" on tumblr

www.ingramcontent.com/pod-product-compliance
Lightning Source LLC
Chambersburg PA
CBHW060609310726
48982CB00003B/504
9780648745402